Mystery
TIMES
NINE
2012

Other Books in This Series

Mystery Times Nine 2012

With Stories by

Kristina L. Martin • Michele Shaw • Wendy Sparrow
KC Sprayberry • Johanna Harness • Sam Hilliard
Melanie Cummins • Donna Jean McDunn
Pat Cox

Edited by MaryChris Bradley

Buddhapuss Ink   Edison NJ

Cover and Book Layout/Design by The Book Team

Library of Congress Control Number: 2012943432

ISBN 978-0-9842035-9-8 (Paperback Original)

First Printing November 2012

PUBLISHER'S NOTE

Buddhapuss Ink LLC and our logos are trademarks of Buddhapuss Ink LLC.

www.buddhapussink.com

Foreword

Buddhapuss Ink continues to strive to live up to our mission to "put our readers first," and this year's edition of *Mystery Times Nine* does just that. All entries were read and rated by judges from our Book Blogger and Teen Panels. The top entries went on to our Editorial Panel, who selected the final nine. Through all of this, our goal was to celebrate those stories that the readers picked as the best.

We received more than one hundred short stories by the final deadline. It was up to our judges to winnow this wealth down to the nine that they felt were the cream of the crop, and the ones they loved are true gems.

To our judges: as always, we couldn't have done this without you. You were amazing, churning through what seemed an endless stack of submissions; you were persistent, demanding, and, we think, dead-on in your picks. Thanks!

To all our entrants we offer a grateful "Thanks!" We enjoyed reading your stories. We laughed, we cried, we were impressed by the quality of your writing. Way to go!

And to our readers: we hope you find this year's picks as entertaining as we have. We gave special notice to the top three winners, but we love them all. Thanks for picking up our humble book!

MaryChris Bradley
Publisher, Buddhapuss Ink LLC

Contents

First Place

Freeing Blue

Kristina L. Martin

DURING DECEMBER, GOVERNOR Joseph Maxwell's house on
Halifax Avenue looked surprisingly like the Governor's Mansion across
the river in St. Paul. Both buildings were built of rock and brick, with a
nod to Tudor architecture, and stood blanketed under two feet of snow.
They each had strings of white lights and wreaths on their wrought-
iron fences, giving the buildings a festive air. But the house on Halifax
had one thing the mansion did not. It had a door on the second floor
that was never, ever left unlocked. And as she sat on the Persian carpet
opening her Christmas presents, it was that door that fourteen-year-old
Maddy kept thinking about.

In no time, Maddy had reduced her stack of presents to torn bits of
shiny paper and a jumbled pile of books, games, and yet another tea set
from her grandmother. Maddy could always count on her grandmother
to give her some kind of teapot or cup. It wouldn't be Christmas without
it. After clearing away the debris, the family gathered in front of the
fireplace and smiled obediently for the photo that would accompany the
annual holiday follow-up letter her grandfather sent to his staff. Then
it was time for Christmas dinner. Each year's meal was the same as the
last: the same roasted goose, side dishes, and desserts. And every year
there was the bickering that turned into an argument. Maddy had no
idea why her mother agreed to make the once-yearly pilgrimage across
town to prove they were still a family, but it was their tradition. After all,
Christmas is a time of family traditions.

"Would it really hurt you, Julia, to spend a bit more time on your
appearance? You'll never get a new husband looking like this. You
have at least an inch of roots showing. Can't you at least try to look
presentable?" Grandmother's annual commentary had waited until the
dessert course this year.

Excusing herself from the table, Maddy went upstairs to use the
bathroom. If she took long enough, Mom wouldn't make her clean her
plate, and they would all blame her lack of appetite on the "excitement"

of the day instead of the ugly words coming from the dining room. Without the buffer of the press, strangers, or hired help, the Maxwells were barely civil to one another. It was Grandmother and Mom who bickered. Grandfather ignored them until he'd drained his third scotch, at which point he joined them.

By the sounds of the clinking glass in the dining room behind her, Maddy decided the scotch was being poured again. Then her grandfather's deep voice rumbled, and the yearly argument was well under way. Maddy could hear snippets of their words, each one chosen for its ability to best wound.

"Merry Christmas," Maddy muttered to herself as she climbed the last of the steps and started down the long hallway. At least the raised voices confirmed she was still alone as she walked down the hallway papered in a subtle blue pattern. Since no one was around to chastise her for leaving behind grease-stained fingerprints, Maddy trailed her fingers along the paper and doorways.

As she walked down the hall, Maddy's footsteps slowed. At the end of the hall were two doors. On the right was the door to the guest bathroom. And on the left was another door that Maddy thought about every time she visited her grandparents. Maddy had the faintest memory of running down the hall to that door long ago. It was a memory colored in pinks and golds, and it made Maddy both happy and sad to remember it. All Maddy knew is that she held her breath and turned the handle every time she was in her grandparents' house, waiting for the unexplained ache of loss to settle in her chest again.

When she reached the bathroom at the end of the hall, she paused and glanced over her shoulder. Confirming she was still alone, she walked over and touched the other doorknob. The brass handle was cold under her fingers. She grasped the knob and turned it, her knuckles brushing against the wood. And for the first time she could remember, the handle turned.

Maddy gasped and pushed the door open a crack. The room was dimly lit by a streetlight at the end of the drive and from some faint light source within. Maddy slid her foot into the room, poking her head around the door as the floor creaked beneath her. The light came from a small lamp sitting on a table beside a twin bed covered in a ruffled comforter and a collection of teddy bears.

Maddy's eyes swept the room and landed on the chair sitting by the window. The girl sitting in the chair was looking at her. She raised a thin, pale hand to Maddy, but before Maddy could speak, her shoulder was caught in a viselike grip.

"Maddy!" her mother hissed. "Come out here right now," she said in a voice Maddy had never heard her mother use before.

"But Mom! Who is she?" Maddy whispered as her mother pulled her into the hallway.

"She's nobody. Now come back downstairs. And not a word of this to anyone." Her mother's voice was a guttural bark pushed from lips gone pale in a madwoman's face. Her mother pushed Maddy toward the stairs, pulling the door shut behind them with a loud click.

Looking back at the door that had been locked for as long as she could remember, Maddy couldn't stop thinking about the girl who seemed so familiar. Whoever she was, Maddy had seen her before.

IN THE WEEKS following Christmas, Maddy tried several times to get her mom to talk about the mysterious girl in her grandparents' house, but it quickly became clear that her mother was not going to talk about the girl or why she was in that room.

"I'm telling you for the last time, Madeline. You are not to ask me another question about that creature again. Have I made myself perfectly clear? You forget about her, do you hear me? Just forget about her or I'm never allowing you in that house again!" her mother screamed at her before running from the room, tears streaming down her face.

But Maddy couldn't forget the way the girl had looked at her, with sad eyes the color of dirty ice, or the way her skin was the same bluish white of marble, as if she were made of stone never kissed by sunlight.

MADDY WAS A tea drinker. Some of her earliest memories were of drinking tea with her grandmother. Whenever there were conflicts between Maddy's parents or their schedules, she wound up drinking a pot of tea with her grandmother.

On Saturday, when her dad's date with his latest girlfriend conflicted with the court-appointed drop-off time, Maddy suggested he let her off at her grandparents' house. As soon as she pointed out he would save gas, time, and avoid a fight with her mom for leaving her unsupervised, he decided it was a brilliant solution. By the time she stepped onto her grandparents' driveway, he acted as if it had been his idea. As he drove off, Maddy smiled at how easy it was to manipulate her dad into letting her have her way.

Of course, manipulating her grandmother would be much, much harder. Maddy could wear down her mother by repeating questions or waiting until she was tired or distracted. But if her grandmother didn't want to let Maddy do something, she simply ignored Maddy's questions or requests until Maddy gave up. The only chink Maddy had ever found in her grandmother's defenses was her fear of what the public would think of the family. Grandmother could always be counted on to choose the route that held up best under public scrutiny.

Later, curled up on the couch, Maddy turned the pages of the musty photo albums and scrapbooks and watched her family grow older, one photo at a time. There were pictures of family vacations, her grandfather when he was the attorney general, and, of course, all of his election photos. Her grandmother commented on some of the photos, and some she only tapped with a perfectly manicured nail. Maddy wasn't sure what the tapping meant, but it must have meant something, because her grandmother's face got sadder as the afternoon passed. Some of the photos were of Julia alone, but most were of her and her twin brother, Joey.

Grandmother paused the longest over one particular photo. It was the four of them when Grandfather was first elected lieutenant governor. He was standing in his old district attorney's office with his arm around Grandmother, and Joey and Julia were next to them.

Grandfather's hair was still dark with only a few streaks of gray at his temples. Grandmother was tiny and perfect, tucked under his arm, and her teenaged mom and uncle looked like poster children for the in-crowd at school. They all looked happy. But less than a year later, Joey was dead. He broke his neck falling down the stairs near where Maddy sat. Maddy figured his death was when their family tradition became one of booze and lies and angry words meant to slowly kill the living.

Sitting there with her grandmother, Maddy asked about the people missing from the collection of photos—namely the generation before the Maxwells had money. For the most part, Grandmother glossed over the details about her own family up in the Iron Range, making them sound like craftsmen instead of miners.

Once or twice Maddy was sure she heard a soft, scraping sound upstairs, as if a chair had slid across the floor. It was so soft a sound that Maddy would have thought she had imagined it except that the lines bracketing Grandmother's mouth deepened each time the sound seeped through the floor.

Maddy didn't necessarily believe in spirits, but it always seemed as if there was something odd about the house on Halifax Avenue. Grandmother refused to leave it, even as Grandfather moved higher and higher on the political ladder. If it had been Maddy, she would have jumped at the chance to move into the Governor's Mansion in St. Paul when Grandfather was elected. But her grandmother insisted they stay where she could remember Joey best. "Besides," Grandmother always said, "I think Edina is a fine place for the governor to live."

Maddy schemed. Finally, Grandmother went into the kitchen to see what the cook had left for dinner and Maddy seized her chance. Quickly, she scribbled a short note on a sheet of paper and folded it into a square. Pocketing the note, Maddy went through the swinging door. As Grandmother moved jars and dishes around the refrigerator shelves, Maddy spied a tub of hummus.

"Hey, Grandmother, do you have any hummus and carrot sticks? I'm starving!"

"I sure do. Would you like some?" her grandmother asked.

"That would be great! Let me run upstairs to the bathroom first though." Maddy tried to keep her voice casual as she smiled up at her grandmother.

Maddy raced up the stairs, taking them two at a time. As she tiptoed down the hallway, Maddy felt her heart pound. A quick glance confirmed that she was alone, so Maddy took out the note. Unfolding it, she smoothed the paper and slid it into the dark space under the door. It laid there, a slice of white paper showing beneath the door.

"Maddy! Hurry up, dear!" her grandmother called from the bottom of the stairs.

Maddy stood there, holding her breath. Finally, Maddy went into the bathroom. And when she came out, the paper was gone.

NEARLY THREE WEEKS passed before Maddy could concoct a good reason to visit her grandparents.

"Mom, remember that family tree project I had to do for English? My teacher liked it so much she wants to keep it as a sample for next year. She said I could get some extra credit if I added my great-great-grandparents. I talked to Oma already for Daddy's side, but now I need your side." Maddy paused, making sure her mom was listening. "Do you know much about your great-grandparents? I need to know their birthdates and stuff like that."

"I have no idea about that. And why on earth do you need extra credit? Haven't you been studying?" Julia's voice hardened until it was a cold knife blade.

"My grades are good; you know that. But you know it never hurts to have a cushion. I thought Grandmother could pick me up after school on Friday, and Dad could drive me to his house after dinner," Maddy said.

Maddy could see Julia thinking through the plan, looking for reasons to say no. But Maddy knew the promise of extra credit would be too much for her mom to resist. Maddy's mom was determined that Maddy would go to college as far from Minnesota as possible. As if Maddy wanted to stay in "Minne-snow-ta" any longer than she had to.

As an only child, Maddy was well trained at reading her parents' body language. With her mom, it didn't take much skill to figure out what she was thinking. It was like watching a storm roll across the prairie. First the storm clouds slipped over the horizon and then they rolled past, leaving a person all kinds of destroyed. Maddy watched wave after wave of emotion flit across her mother's face. Finally Julia rubbed a thin hand across her blue eyes, as if she could rub away whatever bad thoughts filled her mind.

"Sure, whatever. Call your grandmother. I have a headache. I'm going to go lie down. Make yourself some dinner and do your homework."

Julia turned and shuffled down the hallway, her leather slippers scuffing along the hardwood floor. Seeing her mom looking so small and sad, Maddy wondered if learning the mystery girl's identity was worth it.

THE WEATHER TURNED colder as the winter winds came down out of Canada and the temperatures plummeted. It was the kind of Minnesota weather where the wind nearly slices off bits of flesh as it whips past.

When Maddy arrived at her grandparents' house, she immediately started unpacking her school notebooks on the dining-room table. Luckily, the cook had made lots of snacks. Nibbling on them helped

Maddy and her grandmother make notes and lists of relatives without too much small talk about school and boys and "making good decisions." After going through some photos, Grandmother declared they needed to look through one other box.

After she pulled a big box of memorabilia and envelopes of photos from the storage space under the stairs, Grandmother smoothed her blond hair back into its elegantly bobbed haircut and dusted her palms across her wool trousers. Then with a push, she leaned against the closet door until it disappeared with a tiny click. Maddy loved how the closet was hidden in plain sight right there behind the foyer's wainscoting and molding. The locked door upstairs wasn't the only mystery in the house on Halifax Avenue as far as Maddy was concerned.

"Look, Grandmother! It's a ticket stub to *Casablanca*. That must have been awesome to see in the theater," Maddy commented as they sifted through things.

"Oh yes, that has always been one of my favorites. Now, what is this?" her grandmother muttered as she held up an envelope sealed shut. Shrugging, she set it aside.

"Want me to get something to open that?" Maddy offered.

"Sure thing, dear. If she's still here, ask the cook for a pair of scissors."

A quick look in the kitchen proved that the cook had already left for the day. Maddy rifled through the drawers but found no scissors. Then she spied the knife block and grabbed the first handle. Returning to the dining room, she picked up the envelope and started to slit the yellowed paper.

"Oh dear, don't do that. It isn't safe. Here, let me," her grandmother said while she reached for the knife. The older woman started to slip the knife under the flap at the same moment that the garage door opened, signaling that Grandfather had returned. Startled, Grandmother jumped, the knife slicing into the fleshy bit next to her index finger. Hearing her gasp, Maddy looked at her grandmother. Bile rose in her throat when she saw the blade disappearing into her grandmother's hand.

"Oh God, Grandmother!" Maddy gasped, and grabbed the tea towel lying near the teapot.

Her grandmother pulled the knife from her hand and looked at it strangely. Blood welled up and ran down her palm, staining the cuff of her sweater set bright red. Maddy quickly wrapped the towel around the woman's shaking hand while yelling for her grandfather to hurry.

"Maddy, I'll call your mother, and she can come get you," her grandfather yelled over his shoulder as he escorted her grandmother out the door.

"No, my dad is supposed to pick me up!" Maddy shouted to the closing door.

Hearing the car back out of the drive, Maddy took a deep breath before getting a wet cloth from the kitchen to wipe the red dots trailing from the dining room to the garage.

Alone in the house, Maddy was suddenly scared by the possibility of a girl being locked in the room upstairs. Perhaps she was locked up because she was dangerous. And yet Maddy couldn't stop her feet from climbing the stairs. At the door, Maddy reached for the handle but stopped. She stood there listening and counting her heartbeats. Then she sank to the floor beside the door and laid her head on her bent knees. For a long time Maddy sat there, listening to the house creak in the wind. Finally she went back down to the kitchen, opened her notebook to a fresh sheet of paper, and wrote. "Hello. My name is Maddy. What is your name?"

Then she slid the paper under the door into the darkness.

Sliding down to the floor, Maddy laid her head back on her knees and wrapped her arms around her thin legs. Time passed, but Maddy wasn't paying any attention to time. She was too busy listening. She was listening so hard that when the paper slid back toward her, her ear registered the quiet snag of the paper across the carpet long before its edge appeared. When she picked it up, her hand shook.

"Hello Maddy. My name is Josephine. You always called me Blue when we were young."

Maddy dropped the paper with a squeak. Of all the possibilities, reading a response hadn't been one of them. Maddy had all but convinced herself that what she had seen was a ghost. But ghosts can't write. Right? Right. So it must be a real girl behind the locked door. She must be a real girl who wrote those real words on Maddy's notebook paper.

"Blue? I called you Blue? When? What are you talking about?" Maddy nearly shouted at the door.

"You don't remember back then?" a soft voice came from the other side of the door. "Playing with me when you were little? I always wondered if you remembered. You loved to play tea party. That's why Me-maw and I always gave you tea sets. Those were my favorite times, you and I and all my teddy bears—"

"Wait!" Maddy interrupted. "That was real? That was you? I always thought I had an imaginary friend. Mom told me I was only pretending, making up stories; and I guess I believed her," Maddy finished in a choked voice as tears sprang to her eyes.

Bits and pieces of memories filled Maddy's head. She finally remembered hiding in the closet under the stairs with a little girl who looked like a doll, pouring tea for the girl and her teddy bears, playing house. She understood why the locked doorknob always made her heart ache with loss.

She had been about three. Grandmother had offered to watch Maddy while her mother went out. But her mother had come back early and caught Maddy playing with Blue and her grandmother. Her mother had flown into a rage that Blue was there and demanded that Maddy never be around her again. After that, Blue's door was always locked and Grandmother ignored Maddy's pleas to see Blue, until finally Maddy stopped asking.

"Maddy, is she going to be all right? Is Me-maw hurt?" Blue whispered.

Maddy blinked several times until the questions registered in her mind. "Who? Me-maw? Oh, you mean my grandmother? I think so. I mean, of course. She'll be okay."

"Are you sure? I'm so scared. What will I do if she doesn't come back?" Blue's voice broke.

Hearing the girl's sobs, Maddy's heart ached.

"It's going to be okay. Blue, can you open the door?"

"I can't. Me-maw said I could never come out unless she said it was safe," Blue sniffled.

"Of course you can unlock it. It's safe here. I promise its safe. All you have to do is turn the handle. Please, Blue, open the door," Maddy pleaded, her head leaned against the doorjamb.

Slowly, the knob turned until the latch gave way and the door opened a crack. Bit by bit, the door opened until the girl with the marble skin and ice-gray eyes stood before her. She wore a long nightgown strewn with tiny rosebuds, and pink slippers covered her feet. She was a few inches taller than Maddy and had long, white-blond hair cascading down her back. She looked like a porcelain doll come to life.

"Um, hi," Maddy greeted the girl, trying to not stare.

"Hello again, Maddy. You look just the same as you did years ago, except you are bigger, of course. Your hair always makes me think of honey." Blue prattled on the way nervous people sometimes do.

Realizing they were still standing in the doorway, Maddy looked at the blinking girl and then smiled.

"Would you like some tea? Maybe some cookies?" Maddy asked.

Soon, the two girls were seated in the large kitchen, a plate of cookies between them, waiting for the kettle to boil. Maddy was glad she'd wiped Grandmother's blood off the floor earlier.

"Do you still like Constant Comment best, Maddy? Me-maw and I always think of you when we drink it. You couldn't pronounce it when you were little. You called it 'content comma' and so that's what we still call it," Blue said as she sorted through the tea bags. Before Maddy could answer, her cell phone chirped in her jean's pocket.

"Maddy! Oh my God, I'm coming right now to get you!" her mother shouted in Maddy's ear.

"Mom! Mom, you don't need to come get me. Everything is fine," Maddy said into the phone she held away from her ear.

"No, it is absolutely not fine. Your grandfather called me and told me what happened. I'm leaving as soon as I get my coat on."

"Mom, really, it's no big deal. I'll watch some TV until Grandmother gets back or Dad picks me up," Maddy said, trying to keep her voice calm.

"There is no way I'm letting you stay in that house by yourself," her mother said before the phone went silent.

"Crap, my mom is freaking out and coming to get me. It's okay though. It'll take her a while to get here. But we'd better clean up," Maddy smiled at Blue and reached for the plate. Blue rubbed her hand across the table before pushing in her chair. Her face looked so sad.

"What's the matter, Blue?" Maddy asked.

"Nothing really. I wish I didn't have to go back to my room so soon, that's all."

"Why go back? Stay out and wait with me," Maddy said, shocked that Blue would willingly return to her room.

"It's better if I stay there. It isn't very safe for me out here. Not since more and more people started coming to the house during the day.

Someone might see me and try to hurt me. So Me-maw comes in my room or I go in hers," Blue said, a sad smile twisting her lips.

"Wait, you never leave upstairs during the day?" Maddy gasped.

"It's okay; I don't mind," Blue murmured, avoiding the question, carrying her cup and saucer to the sink.

"Okay, that's messed up, Blue. You don't need to hide away from people, just because you look…" Maddy stopped, unsure how to continue. "Uh, your real name is Josephine, right? That's pretty cool. My uncle was Joseph. Well, he went by Joey because my grandfather goes by Joseph," Maddy casually mentioned as she stacked the plates and threw away the wet tea bags.

"Yes. Me-maw says I'm just like him. She says I'm special like he was. But even more special because of my skin," Blue smiled and waved one of her milky-white hands.

Maddy squinted at the girl standing next to her. It was hard to guess her age because Blue was so pale and acted so childlike. Maddy thought about Blue's skin and her pale eyes.

"Special like how, besides being, uh, is it okay to say 'albino' or is that like bad? That's why your skin is so pale, right? You're an albino?" Maddy said in a rush, her face turning hot.

"I don't know what 'albino' means. Me-maw says I'm special because I am a caulbearer. Both Joseph and I are caulbearers. In some families, that happens. Me-maw says it means we were both marked by God to be extraordinary!" Blue finished with an angelic smile.

"So I guess Joey was your dad, which would make you my cousin. But what happened to your mother?" Maddy puzzled over the facts Blue had laid out so matter-of-factly.

"I don't know my mother. All I know is Me-maw. God gave me to Me-maw because she missed Joseph so much her heart was about to break. So I came, and Me-maw was able to smile again."

Maddy decided to ignore most of Blue's explanation. Church was one thing Maddy didn't spend much time thinking about. But Maddy couldn't let go of Blue having been held captive in the house all these years.

"But why do they keep you locked up? Grandmother, er, Me-maw can be kinda weird, but that seems too farout there even for her. And what was that word you said? Call something or other. I don't know that word."

"Caulbearers must be protected, so she had to keep me hidden for my own protection. People are always trying to hurt caulbearers because they are jealous. And they try to steal us or our cauls to keep them safe from drowning or to steal our luck. Bad people do all sorts of terrible things."

"But what is a caul?" Maddy asked again. Some small part of the conversation bothered her, but she couldn't quite figure out what it was so she ignored it.

"It is a gift from God, Maddy! It is a very special veil only truly blessed children are born with. It's a part of the bag of waters that surround a baby before it is born, but we caulbearers are born with it still covering our faces. Like a veil, you see? We are veiled from sight, like an angel from God."

Listening to Blue talk about being born with a caul, Maddy realized what was bothering her. "Blue, how long have you lived here?"

"Oh, my whole life. I was born here, seventeen years ago, right in the room I live in. Me-maw has kept my caul and me safe all these years. Safe from all the people who would want to hurt me or steal my caul," Blue said.

"You still have it?" Maddy couldn't keep the revulsion from her voice, but Blue didn't notice.

"Yes! Me-maw saved it for me. I can show you, if you'd like," Blue offered, turning as if to leave the room.

"That's okay, maybe later. Do you know what happened to your mother? How did she come to live with my grandmother?" Maddy asked, her brow wrinkled.

"I don't know, but I can show you a picture of her. It's right by my bed, where I can pray for her and Joseph."

The girls went back upstairs, and Blue proudly pointed to her collection of teddy bears. Next to her bed was a small table with a clock and a stack of books. And sitting between the lamp and the bed was a framed photograph.

It was the photograph of Maddy's family, taken after her grandfather won his first election.

"See, wasn't she beautiful?" Blue picked up the frame and tapped the glass over Julia's face.

Maddy stood there, clutching the photo. In the distance there was a slamming sound, but she barely noticed it. Instead, Maddy focused on the face of her mother, smiling up at her. The feet running down the hall got louder and louder until her grandfather spun her around to face him.

"What are you doing in here!" he roared at her before shaking her by both shoulders. He continued to yell and shake her until it felt as if her head would surely come off.

"You stupid, stupid girl. You had to keep messing with things that are none of your business, and now look what you've done!" he yelled before pushing Maddy from him. Turning to look down at the pale girl crouched on the floor, he pointed a long finger at her and said in a very quiet and controlled voice, "Go get in your chair. Now! And you'd better not make a sound. Do you understand me?"

Both girls whimpered at the rage in his voice. Instead of standing up, Blue slid backward until she bumped into the chair and then she crept her way into it, huddled in a small ball with her legs pulled against her chest.

Seeing her grandfather's attention was moving from the girl in the chair back to her, Maddy tried to scramble across the bed, but the headboard stopped her.

Pointing his finger at her, he muttered, "I've worked too damn hard to get where I am to have you mess things up. You are just like your mother. Always worried about yourself and what you want. Well, let me tell you something; I'm not letting you ruin things for me. I will teach you to keep your mouth shut."

And he walked toward the bed.

"Stop right there, Father. This is over. You touch her, and it will be the last thing you do," Julia said through tight lips. The gun in her hand was still as she pointed it at her father.

"Mom?" Maddy gasped.

"You okay, Maddy? Did he hurt you? Because if he did, I think I may pull this trigger right now."

"No, I'm okay. We're okay. But thank God you got here so fast," Maddy said.

"Looks like the truth is out, isn't it, Father? All these years you tried to keep everything a secret, but it looks like you can't hide the truth any longer. Now move away from her." Julia gestured with the gun barrel to the wall near the closet.

Raising his hands and moving a few inches toward the wall, Joseph's voice was smooth, like someone soothing a stray cat.

"Everything is going to be fine, Julia. I can take care of everything. I—"

"Take care of everything like the way you took care of Joey? He found out what you'd been doing to me for years, and look how you took care of him, pushing him down the stairs. And the baby you left me with, look how well you took care of her. You said you'd make sure she had a good home, and instead you gave her to Mother as if she's some kind of doll to play with in secret. Your days of taking care of things are over," Julia interrupted.

Joseph's face darkened, and he dropped his hands and crept toward Julia.

"Are you trying to threaten me, Julia, because that would be a mistake. I don't like threats. You know what happened the last time you threatened me," he whispered, walking closer and closer to Julia until he stopped short of the gun barrel. "Now give me the gun before you make a fool of yourself."

Maddy slowly connected what was being said. She suddenly realized that the years of Christmas arguments were really about one thing: lies designed to keep the second-floor bedroom on Halifax Avenue a secret. In that instant, everything Maddy thought she knew about her family changed.

Suddenly, Grandfather lunged at Maddy's mom and smacked the gun out of her hand. The gun clattered on the floor, and a figure rushed toward it.

Blue stood there, holding the gun in her pale, pale hands.

"Me-maw said bad people would come someday and try to hurt me. She said that I must be careful and be very, very quiet or the bad people would find me. But she never said they would be you."

• • •

STANDING AT THE graveside, Maddy stood between her parents, gripping their hands. It had snowed the night before, making the cemetery sparkle in the weak sunshine. Everything was white and clean. As the dirt clattered across the casket, Maddy thought about how much had changed since the morning she opened her tea set on Christmas morning.

Across town, sitting in a hard chair, Blue's eyes, colored like the ice on

Lake Minnetonka, filled with tears; but she made no sound. After years of being silent, Blue was good at crying without making any sounds. Even freed from her room, she was still trapped in silence.

KRISTINA L. MARTIN: Giving life to the stories in her head/heart became an active part of her daily life a few years ago when she started blogging and then became a professional stand-up comic. Her writing evolved from "just a blogger" to an essayist and now novelist. Kristina's first novel, *The Blue Dress*, is a young adult historical, and she's currently working on a second young adult novel: a contemporary thriller. She updates her blog, Ten Minute Missive, on Mondays and Fridays and can be found most days on Twitter as @quickmissive.

Second Place

A Shot in the Dark

Michele Shaw

IT DIDN'T MATTER that I'd always hated skiing. Having it taken away seemed unfair. That's what I thought when we drove past the slopes on the first day of winter break. Chairs filled with skiers climbed the hill like ants on a conveyor belt. I wanted to ride with them and hop off, flying down at top speed. But only because I couldn't.

Minutes later, we navigated the final turn to our weekend cabin, sliding to a stop in front of the place where everything had changed. I'd played it over in my mind a million times. If only we'd chosen the beach last year, I'd have tanned, working legs. My dad would still be alive.

I stared ahead at the fresh snow, somehow surprised that the pools of blood had disappeared. Gone were the big one that had spread from underneath Dad, leaching into the frozen white like a cherry sno-cone and the smaller ones that had trailed after Mom as she ran into the woods.

I'd memorized it all as they wheeled me out on a gurney, though the scene had multiplied and twisted as if I was squinting through a kaleidoscope. A man in navy draped something over my father's face while red and blue lights circled, bouncing off him. Another man took pictures of crimson footprints. Each stunted breath had burned and stabbed at my chest as I tried to make sense of it before I lost consciousness.

"Look, Mare," said Mom, pointing forward. "Uncle Jim built a ramp for you."

I turned and glared. We'd talked about the name, but she kept forgetting.

"Yes, yes. I know. I'm sorry. I meant to say Marritt, but look."

The glare was bratty for someone in high school and I knew it, but this whole trip felt pointless. Why did we need to come back here? Why hadn't she sold the cabin? Or even burned it down? I didn't want to look at, touch, or even smell the place where an intruder flipped a switch in his mind and decided our fates: Dad gone, Mom a widow, and me paralyzed. All for some jewelry and a little cash.

The ramp started to the left and crossed the stairs, doing a U-turn and ending at the deck. A wedge rested over the step into the door.

"I can't make it," I said, lowering my chin.

"You can. You just need to try." She grabbed my hand, with hers trembling as our fingers laced together. "I've been thinking about giving the cabin to Jim. Would you mind that? He spent his childhood here with Dad."

I stared into the pines surrounding us and the mountain jutting from behind our A-frame's peak. The view made it hard to believe something so horrible had happened here. But it had, and nothing could change that.

"No. Do it now. You know I don't want to be here. Aren't you scared?"

She nodded. "A little, but Jim installed a security system. And…I think if we turn and run away, the bad guy wins. Your dad wouldn't want that."

She gave my hand a squeeze and got out. The outside air rushed through her door, and the sting of burning wood hit my nostrils. Swirling gray smoke puffed from the chimney at the side of the cabin, calming me some. A sign Jim had been here within the last hour. His own place sat just a mile down the road.

I took a slow breath and let it leak back out. Only a weekend, two days—I could do that one last time.

The trip in went smoother than I'd thought, thanks to the ramp. My arms responded to the challenge, the months of therapy finally paying off. I rolled to a stop in the doorway. Going all the way in weighed on my shoulders and squeezed my throat. I glanced up, expecting the roof to cave in from the heaviness in the air.

Our gold rug had disappeared, filled with glass shards and blood spatter—my blood, from a shot in the back when I'd tried to run up the stairs. An ugly brown recliner, Dad's favorite, was gone too. The empty spot turned my stomach. Mom breezed past and pulled the shade on the kitchen window.

"We need some light in here." She walked the perimeter of the main room, flicking on lights and adjusting knick-knacks that some well-meaning person had placed off their normal spots by an inch or two: the statue of a mother bear with her cub, the cabin replica I'd made for

Dad from Popsicle sticks in first grade.

"I thought I'd give you the master, and I'll take the loft. The bath down here is bigger anyway. It should work out great."

Yeah, great. The size of the bedroom wouldn't dull the screaming in my head. Or the urge to get as far away from here as possible. But I didn't speak, instead just nodding while she went to get our bags. I wanted to wallow alone.

I rolled into my new room and steeled myself for what I knew I'd find. Pictures of Dad. Of us, so different. Him, alive and vibrant. Me, with the full use of my body. Mom, with fewer stress lines and a lightness to her smile. Twelve months ago that was us.

I rolled past the pictures on the dresser, unable to look, and stared at the deer head on the wall opposite the bed. How was I supposed to sleep with that thing watching me all night? I hated hunting, which had disappointed my "king-of-the-hunters" dad. I hurt at the thought but couldn't help it. If I were only bigger, stronger…a boy. Maybe a son could have protected him, overtaken the intruder. Saved his life.

Of all his belongings, I'd only wanted to keep his favorite: a pocketknife. I fished for it in my coat and rubbed my thumb along the worn spot on the handle, remembering him explaining the blood zone and how to use it safely. No problem for me; I had no plans to use it. But I felt closer to him with it in my pocket.

Voices other than Mom's carried across the cabin. I startled and turned.

"Marritt. Look who's here," Mom called.

I rolled to the doorway. Mr. and Mrs. Fox, our closest neighbors, stood in the living room. Their cabin sat halfway between ours and the one Jim had built for himself a few years back. They'd persuaded Dad and Jim to sell them the land for Fox Hollow, their dream cabin, and had finally finished construction last year.

Mrs. Fox rushed to me with a potted African violet in her hand. Her bubble parka swish-swished as she walked. She set the plant in my lap and hugged my shoulders.

"It's so wonderful to see you, hon. You look fabulous."

"Betty, let the girl breathe," said Mr. Fox, holding his hand out in a chopping motion. "We're not staying. Just wanted to make sure you gals were okay and settled in."

"Thank you," I said in nearly a whisper. I righted the tipping plant and brushed some dirt from my jeans.

"Let me just set that on the counter," said Mrs. Fox with a flush to her cheeks. She held the pot under the sink, dripping water into the soil. "You remember my son Zane? He's the one who found your mom and called for help."

I turned back to Mr. Fox. He slapped the shoulder of a boy who'd walked in next to him and who stood every bit of his more than six feet. I'd never seen him before that I remembered. Brown curly hair, a junior or maybe a senior like me. He held up his hand and half smiled.

"No, I don't remember. Sorry."

"Don't be," said Zane. "Mom, we've never met."

"Really?" Mrs. Fox asked, setting the pot in the window before washing her hands. "I could've sworn you had. Well, my oldest, Jack, should be here in a few hours. He's driving up with some of his college friends. I'm putting that loud bunch out in the guest cottage. Let me tell you…"

"They don't need the whole story," said Mr. Fox as he guided his wife to the door. "You have our number," he said to Mom. "If the snow picks up again, I'll send one of the boys over to clear the ramp."

Mom held the door with one hand and shook Mr. Fox's with the other. "I don't know that I've ever properly thanked you."

"Not necessary. Call anytime." He nodded, and they walked out.

She shut the door and turned, leaning against it.

"So, he's the one," I said. "The kid who found you."

"Yes. I'm grateful every day that he did, but it still bothers me."

"What does?"

She moved to sit by the fire. After several seconds of staring past me, she shook her head, looking toward her lap. "I could see the lights from their windows. They seemed miles away, and my voice wouldn't work. I fought so hard not to fall, but the blood loss and the snow…if I'd made it. If you and Dad had gotten help sooner."

"Mom, don't," I said as she covered her face and sobbed into her hands. I tried to roll next to her, but my chair wouldn't fit between the couch and the fireplace. I shoved as hard as I could. The stupid, heavy couch wouldn't move. I shoved again and again, letting out a shriek and breaking into a sweat. Months of anger exploded from my arms, but the couch still wouldn't budge. I back up, turned, and rolled into my new room. The door slammed when I whipped it closed. And I cried until I couldn't anymore.

• • •

I CHRISTENED THE deer head Larry. After staring at him all night, it felt as if we were friends. His nose shone like wet leather, and the brownish-black orbs that stood in for his eyes followed me everywhere. I asked him what he'd seen. What he knew. Who had done this to us, and why they hadn't been caught? He didn't answer.

It took an hour to haul myself from the bed to the chair, into the bathroom, and get through my morning routine. Mom was right about the extra space giving me enough room to maneuver. I eyed the jet tub but opted to give myself a sponge bath. If Mom had to help me, she'd want to talk; and after last night, I didn't have the energy.

I managed to stuff my hair into a ponytail and put in my favorite earrings: diamond studs Dad had given me for my sixteenth birthday. I felt lucky to have left them at home last year. The intruder took everything we'd had with us at the time, including Mom's rings and the diamond solitaire necklace she wore. It held the stone from my grandmother's wedding ring.

Bacon and eggs pulled me to the kitchen, and I sped up when Jim stood from the table. He rushed to meet me halfway and bear-hugged me. Jim was ten years younger than my dad, a bachelor, and the most interesting person I knew.

"My Fair Mare. You look ready for action. Good thing. I've got a little something planned for today," he said, winking.

"Whatever it is, the answer is no," I said. I knew it couldn't be good. As much as my dad had wanted me to hunt, Jim wanted me to be adventurous. I was an utter failure at it with the hospital record to prove it. There was the broken arm from when he'd put me on a four-wheeler and the stitches from a rock-climbing mishap, to name a few.

"Just hold on," Mom said, sitting with her coffee. "We have something else to tell her first, don't we?" Her eyes had mellowed, and her posture had loosened. Maybe because of her purge from the night before.

"Right." He patted my shoulder and pushed me to the table. "You eat. I'll talk."

I filled my plate, dreading what I was about to hear. As much as I didn't want to be in the cabin, I'd planned to pass the weekend reading and drawing. I knew any plot of Jim's involved going outside.

"So, Mare." Mom tapped his arm and he cleared his throat. "Oh, right. Marritt. As far as giving up the cabin, I understand. It's hard for me too. But I'd like to keep it. My dad built the place. I won't just let you two hand it to me though. I'm going to buy it and then your mom is going to buy you a car. One with hand controls. You, my girl, are going to drive again." He pointed at me and pulled that grin I knew so well. The one that told me I was doing whatever he said.

"D-driving? Are you kidding? I only drove a few times the regular way. I can barely dress myself."

He sighed and ran his hand over his head. "Excuses. I don't want to hear 'em. Think about independence. Driving your friends around, or if you want to be practical, maybe you could get a job, help your mom run errands. I know you'd like to think so, but you're not an invalid."

I pinched my lips, then blew out a breath to relax. Jim could be a chigger under my skin when he chose, but I had to admit he was usually right. But a job? Helping Mom? Things I'd never considered. All I'd been for the last twelve months was a burden. And most of the time, a grouchy, complaining one at that.

The door rattled from a knock, and Jim jumped to get it.

"Morning," he said to Zane. "She's almost ready."

I dropped my fork, looking between the three of them for an answer. Zane wiped his feet and stood by the door. He had goggles perched on a white ski hat, and his cheeks were flushed.

"No hurry," he said. "It's all set." He flashed a grin, then bent to fix the buckle on one of his boots.

"Who's going to tell me?" I asked.

Mom held up her palms and walked to the sink. Jim grabbed a hat and planted it on my head, covering my eyes.

"Let's get you suited up. You're going snowmobiling today."

• • •

JIM AND ZANE had modified the snowmobile with a backrest. They'd also fashioned a harness for me out of leather that had a belt that wrapped around Zane. After anchoring my knees with straps that attached to Zane's belt, Jim told me to lean forward, grab Zane's waist, and hang on. My protests were ignored as they adjusted and twisted me as if I was a mannequin.

"I'm not doing this!" I finally yelled.

Jim laughed and put his hand to his ear. Zane revved the snowmobile as Jim mouthed, "Can't hear you."

I wanted to give him the finger, but Zane took off, and I held on with all I had. The only thing that kept me from screaming was Zane's head so close to mine. But the dips and hills caused a few yelps as snow flew past us and bit my cheeks. When we reached a clearing, it leveled out and we picked up speed. Cold air burned down my throat as I tried to snuffle in the drips from my nose before they stuck to my face.

Clear blue above pressed an ache on my heart. Just as clear as that day a year ago. Dad and I had gone hiking. We took pictures and talked about colleges along the way. The best day we'd had in a while. No arguing about grades or the softball practice I had ditched to go to the mall.

We'd returned just before dinner to a dark house. The intruder already had Mom on the floor, the gun pressed to her head. Then he'd pointed from one of us to the other as he shouted for us to give him our money and get down. He had a black mask, full coverage, like for skiing. Brown hair; just a few wisps hung from the bottom. They were wiry and shiny, possibly a wig. I'd repeated it to the police many times. Tall, thin, black clothes, brown hair. No, I didn't recognize the voice. No, I didn't see what color his eyes were.

Zane slowed as we took a narrow trail through the woods that eventually brought us to the parking lot of The Junction, the local hangout, supply store, bar, restaurant, everything place. He turned off the motor and glanced over his shoulder.

"Want to break for hot chocolate? I need to get gas."

As good as that sounded, I had no way to get in, which I thought seemed obvious. But I didn't want to call him stupid. I enjoyed the idea that maybe for one second he forgot I needed the chair.

"Sure. I'll wait here."

"No, you won't."

He undid the belt, then turned, wrangling the harness and straps off. I held one hand on his shoulder for balance.

"I have to," I said, pulling my hand away and crossing my arms. "In case you didn't notice, it's at least thirty feet to the store, and I count ten steps in."

"Well, aren't you the math wiz. Figure this." He reached under my shoulders and legs, lifting me with ease, and started toward the store. "I'd say you're five two and about a hundred pounds. I'm six two and one eighty. I think I can handle it."

He had guessed close to perfect. I'd weighed more last year when I pitched for my softball team, ran, and had more muscle in my legs.

He climbed the steps and took me in to a table near the fire. "Marshmallows?" he asked after settling me in a chair.

"Obviously."

He laughed and walked to the counter.

Only two other people occupied the seating area, whispering and darting their eyes toward me every few seconds. I recognized them: the Jensens. Jim didn't like them, calling them mountain wannabes. They used their cabin for wild parties with their wealthy friends but never actually skied, or hiked, or did anything outdoorsy. Mrs. Jensen wore a vest made of some kind of fur, and her neck dripped in gold chains. Mr. Jensen sported a crisp green sweater. I had to hold in a laugh when I spotted a price tag dangling from the sleeve of the new parka draped over his chair.

Zane returned with two cups. They overflowed with marshmallows that tumbled out and bounced to the floor as he walked.

"You went overboard. I thought you could count," I said.

"I can, smart-ass. Margie's working the counter."

"Oh, right." Margie had worked at The Junction as long as I could remember. Whenever you ordered anything, she served it in lumberjack portions. "Since you already think I'm a smart-ass, mind if I ask why you're doing this? I'm sure you'd rather be somewhere else than hauling a cripple around."

"I don't mind," he said, shrugging his shoulder. "Jim asked."

I looked to the table, surprised at the disappointment I felt. I knew that would be his answer; but some little part of me—the part that had noticed how strong his arms were under me and how sweet his smile was, and mostly the way he didn't talk to me like a two-year-old—wanted him to see me as a girl. A regular, fully functional girl and not someone he was arm-twisted into spending the day with.

"I know that. I guess I just wandered how much he paid you."

His brow crinkled, and he shook his head. "He asked, and I said yes because I'd do anything for him. He's helped me a lot this year. Every weekend we've been up here, I've talked to him about…ya know."

"Why would you want to talk about that?"

"I've felt…bad. About your dad and wishing I had found your mom sooner. I was out goofing around on the snowmobile. I was late getting back home for dinner. If I'd been on time…"

He sounded just like Mom. Blaming and what-ifing himself to death. They both sounded like me, though I'd hidden my guilt and shame. His words hit me like a smack to the temple. I'd let the last year become all about me and my injury, not realizing how much that day had affected everyone, and I felt like a jerk.

"You shouldn't," I said, reaching my hand across the table. I yanked it back when the overbearing stench of flowers and musk hit my nose.

Mrs. Jensen touched her French manicure fingernails to my arm. "We were so sorry about your father. We sent flowers."

I glanced at her eyes, so blue that they had to be colored contacts, then turned back to Zane. "Thanks. They were very nice."

She stepped away, and Zane stood, leaving his cup.

"I'll go fill up and then come back for you."

• • •

OUR TRIP HOME went perfectly as I relaxed into the harness and rode with confidence. Zane didn't complain that I squeezed him too tight—as he had in the morning—and didn't say a word when I rested my tired head against him.

When we arrived at the cabin, he undid all the straps and carried me to the door. Mom opened it before I reached for the knob. Her puffy, red eyes looked sunken and defeated, but she threw on a smile and pulled the door wide.

"Well, look at those cheeks. I'd say the fresh air did you some good. You're not angry with Jim, are you?"

"I guess not. He's safe for now." I looked up at Zane, our faces close enough to send heat to my cheeks. To make it worse, I had to ask something I'd rather not. "Can you get me to my bedroom? I have to get out of some of these layers."

The phone rang, and Mom went to get it, pointing the way for him as she went. He carried me across the living room and turned sideways in the door before setting me on the bed.

"There you go, heavyweight. You're bulking up my pitching arm."

I sat back, pulled off my hat, and unzipped my coat. "First of all, I'm not heavy, but you play baseball? Pitcher?"

"Yeah. Hoping to get a scholarship. You like baseball?"

Pain seared behind my eyes, and I squeezed them tight. "Softball. I used to play." I turned my head toward the dresser and the last team picture I was in. My solo picture in the yellow-and-white Jaguars uniform sat to its right.

He followed my gaze and walked to it. "Pitcher?" he asked.

I nodded with a tear trailing toward my ear. He turned back and stared for a second.

"Bet you were good. They must suck without you."

I couldn't help smiling though my chin quivered. Sweat sprouted on my neck as the warm cabin closed in around me.

He walked over and helped me out of the coat, then stared at my ski pants. "Uh, you need help with…"

As embarrassing as it was, the overbearing heat won out. I took a deep breath. "I'll unzip, if you'll tug from the heels?"

He pulled as I held the waist of my sweats. After the pants slid to the floor, he straightened and looked away awkwardly. I knew another dose of my reality had to be hitting him. He'd done the favor for Jim, and now he was clear. I figured I might as well say *"Nice knowing you, Zane. Run away now. I know you want to."*

"Well, I should go."

Perfect timing. Just as I thought. "Okay. Thanks for the ride."

"Sure." He turned to the door but stopped and turned back. "Listen, my brother and his friends are having a bonfire later. If you want to go, I could come back and get you. Around six?"

The invitation took a minute to register. Had I heard him right? This didn't sound like part of his promise to Jim.

"Well?" he finally asked when I sat there silent like an idiot.

"Uh…okay. Maybe for a while. Can you drive that thing in the dark?"

"Just wait," he said, grinning wide, "you have no idea."

• • •

MOM JUMPED WITHOUT hesitation when I asked her to help me with a bath in the afternoon. She washed my hair and combed through all the tangles. Having something useful to do seemed to make her happy. She left, looking confused when I refused her help getting dressed, something I'd rarely done in my year as a helpless baby. She walked out, saying she needed to start cooking anyway.

Jim joined us for dinner and we chatted, even talking about the worst day of our lives without anyone crying. I was starting to think Mom had it right. Maybe this trip would heal us a little, and when we left the cabin, we'd be stronger.

"Sheriff Dawley says the case isn't closed; they just don't have any new leads, but you never know," Jim said through a mouthful of potatoes.

"I should call him," Mom said. "I took a walk earlier, and I thought of something. I don't know why it hit me suddenly. That day, in the morning, we found wild snowmobile tracks around the house and liquor bottles. We threw out the bottles and figured the tracks must have been some drunken guests of the Jensens. Whoever it was didn't know how to drive. Why would I have forgotten that? So stupid." She stared into space, and Jim touched her arm.

"It's not stupid. You were shot twice and left for dead. I don't know how you made it as far as you did. Anyway, they cleared everyone at that party. Bunch of high idiots but not murderers. Still, you should call him."

She nodded as the roar of Zane's snowmobile grew. His lights swept across the window.

"I guess that's for me." I rolled to the coatrack and gathered my things. Mom helped me into everything while Zane and Jim talked curfew and snowmobile safety at night.

With two practice runs behind us, Zane had me strapped in, and we set off in minutes. Even through sweaters and whatever else he had on, he smelled fresh, sort of earthy. I knew I wasn't the only one who'd bathed. My loose hair blew behind me, the wind burning my nose and ears the whole way.

We pulled through the trees just behind Fox Hollow, where a huge fire roared in a circle of stones near the guest cottage. Benches made from logs served as seats for the two girls and three guys with blankets over their legs. They laughed and passed a bottle as the flame's reflection danced across their faces. It was easy to pick out Jack: a slightly older, bulkier version of Zane.

Zane undid my contraption and carried me to a blanket he'd laid on a tarp. If the others didn't know about my lack of leg power when we pulled up, they did now. I'd agreed to the outing on an impulse, forgetting how my condition turned a party into a room full of awkward. Marritt Baker: official buzz killer. People would tense up, look away, and stumble over their words. If I'd given it any thought, I would have said no; but now I was stuck with a group of strangers who'd stopped laughing and gone mute the minute I'd arrived.

Jack dove in first, finally breaking the silence. "Hey, I'm Jack. Sorry about your dad."

I nodded, hoping to get off the subject as he pointed around the circle. "Baldy, Jen, Matt, and my girl, Sadie," he said, stopping at the girl next to him.

They all mumbled something like "Hey" or "Hi" and returned to passing the bottle. Zane propped a pillow against the log behind me and helped me scoot back against it. He sat next to me on the blanket.

The one called Baldy—which I didn't understand because he had a full head of long blond hair pulled into a ponytail—lit a cigarette and laughed as the smoke billowed out.

"Nice, Zane. Can you find any more excuses to grab her?" He coughed on the smoke and put his hand up to deflect the rock Jack had tossed at him.

"Shut up, asshole, or this is the last time I'm inviting you up here," said Jack.

"Oh, come on, J. They know I'm kidding." He flicked the lit cigarette at Jack, who in turn picked it up and smoked it with a smile. Baldy took the bottle from Jen, a skinny girl in a yellow parka who had two black braids hanging from her matching hat. Her smile had a weird angle to it, as if she wasn't fully in control of her mouth, and her hazy eyes made her look half asleep.

The one Jack called Matt sat next to Jen, eyeing his boots. He glanced up a time or two but looked back down when he saw me watching. His was more the type of reaction I expected: the "Oh, no, what do I say to a cripple?" look.

"She's cute, lover boy," said Sadie. "You've certainly done worse."

Jack laughed and wrapped his arm around her.

Zane turned as if he was looking over his shoulder, but leaned in and whispered, "Jeez, sorry. I don't know why Jack hangs with these losers. He's lucky my parents haven't figured out they're always wasted. You're probably ready to go now, right?"

He was so embarrassed, it was kind of cute. He had no idea that this wasn't any worse than the way strangers usually treated me, and it was far more entertaining. Besides, I felt a certain power I hadn't in months. He needed my comfort, not the other way around.

"Are you kidding?" I whispered back. "I can see this is going to get good."

He turned to me and smiled. "Okay. For a while. But let me know when you get cold. Jim will kill me if you get frostbite."

I nodded, and we both stared into the fire as it crackled back to life when Jack poked the logs.

After that, everyone but poor Matt seemed not to notice we were there. I felt kind of sorry for him. He was clearly the odd man out as the others shared the occasional grope and kiss. The few times he glanced my way, he turned as soon as our eyes met. Before long, he'd downed half a bottle on his own, spending the rest of the time scraping a pocketknife across a twig.

I tried to ignore him and keep my attention on Zane. We talked about baseball, our fastest pitches, how our teams had placed. We talked about where we might go to school. I didn't want to explain how far behind I'd gotten and that even though I was technically a senior, I might have to go an extra semester. But it was nice being with him anyway. I almost felt normal.

Jack and Sadie had settled in a sleeping bag, looking as if they had passed out after the second bottle emptied. Baldy and Jen got louder and stupider as time wore on. Jen danced and nearly stumbled into the fire. "The coat has got to go," she yelled, stripping it off and twirling it over her head.

Zane leaned over. "Here we go. You called it right."

I laughed, turning back to see what she would do next. When she spun in my direction, the light from the fire hit it: a flash of white that passed in a second. Jen swayed her hips, a motion I would normally be jealous of, but I couldn't take my eyes off the diamond rocking side to side on a chain around her neck. A large solitaire, just like the one stolen from my mother.

I told myself lots of people owned diamond necklaces. It didn't mean anything. But my mom's setting was unique; a curved piece of gold wrapped each side, but no prongs held it—a floating diamond, they called it. Not one of a kind but definitely not typical.

As the stone moved in and out from under her collar with each of her movements, I watched it like the pendulum on a grandfather clock. Glimpses of the familiar shape became clearer each time. The top half of my body grew as useless as the bottom. I couldn't take my eyes off Jen, and I couldn't speak.

Zane touched his glove to mine. "You look cold. You okay?"

"I need to go," I managed to whisper, trying not to make it come out as a hiss. "I need to go now." Jen moved and sat on Baldy's lap. I felt as if the fear had to be written on my face, coming off in waves and hitting everyone around me. After a hard swallow, I tried to relax my jaw and ease my shoulders.

"Yeah, sure," said Zane with his brow pulled.

"Hurry, okay?"

He nodded, looking confused, and I figured he thought I might pee all over myself or something. At least I hoped it was anything other than the truth.

He ran to the snowmobile and started it, then hurried back and scooped me up under my arms and legs.

Baldy and Jen were engrossed in a makeout session but separated when Matt jumped and pulled Baldy's arm. He whispered in Baldy's ear, and they argued.

My pulse jumped so high, I was getting dizzy.

Zane had me on the seat and had started to get the harness on when Baldy walked up with Matt behind him.

I turned to see Jack still fast asleep with Sadie. I wanted to scream, but for all I knew, he was with them. Then I realized that even Zane might be with them, but that thought fled as quickly as it had come. None of this made sense anyway. I only remembered one intruder.

"Where you rippin' off to? Party's just getting started. Your girl got a problem?" asked Baldy. Matt shifted his weight nervously.

Zane kept going with the straps. My shoulders quivered against the backrest, but I held up my arms so he could finish. "It's getting cold, and she has a curfew. Go maul your wasted girlfriend some more." He turned and sat on the seat, grabbing the straps from my legs to hook them.

"I told you we shouldn't have come back. She knows. We gotta get out of here. I'm not down for any more of this," said Matt.

"Shut up!" Baldy screamed over his shoulder. "Look, little man, we need to talk. You're not going anywhere." He grabbed Zane's shoulder, but Zane shook him off. "Get her," Baldy said to Matt.

Matt shook his head but started toward me as Baldy pulled a pistol from his waistband. He lowered it just inches from Zane's head.

"What are you doing?" screamed Jen from her place by the fire.

"Stay there," Baldy yelled to her without moving the gun.

Zane didn't have my legs strapped in, but the belt was around his waist. I grabbed him just before we heaved to the left. He leaned and power-kicked Baldy in the knee, then righted us and revved the motor. We took off as a hand grabbed my collar. Matt yanked it hard; but the pull stopped when we moved, and I flung forward against Zane.

He left the lights off, heading into the trees by moonlight. A shot cracked past, and we ducked our heads but kept going.

"I hear motors," I yelled in his ear. "They're following us."

"I can outrun them, just keep your head down," he yelled back.

Though they were a ways behind, their headlights tossed shadows through the trees when I craned around. I turned, burying my face in Zane's coat. We hit a bump, and I yelped. My right leg bounced off, dragging my boot through the snow. I hadn't felt it but looked down when my balance was thrown.

"Zane, my leg."

He slowed and looked back. The lights grew closer, but he hoisted my leg and hurried to attach the straps. When he turned to start again, the engine died. "Come on, come on," he said, flicking switches and hitting the button. The whine of their engines grew. I didn't know what to do, so I took off one glove and dug under my coat into my hoodie. The warm pocketknife met my shaking fingers. I pulled it out, letting the small stream of moonlight that broke the trees gleam off the steel edge. The hard knife felt foreign, and I wondered if I could really thrust it at someone.

The snowmobile started on the third try, so I shoved the knife back into my coat pocket. We took off again with lights this time as the path narrowed. The trees became dense in the last stretch before the clearing to my cabin. Shouts echoed across the frozen night. Zane sped up. Another shot cracked, then a second one, and Zane's left arm flew to his neck.

"Are you hit?" I shouted. But he didn't respond or move his hand.

We pulled up in front of the cabin. All the lights were out. A thousand thoughts passed through my mind in less than a second. Where were Mom and Jim? She wouldn't be asleep, would she? What time was it? Was Zane still breathing? How would he get me off this thing if he was hurt?

Zane stopped and slumped to the side. We both fell into the snow. I tried to call out but only choked out a rasp even I couldn't hear. I shook Zane's shoulder, which covered my glove with blood. Lights swept over us, and I laid my head against Zane, hoping to at least keep him warm. I searched my right pocket, pulling out the knife and hitting the button with my hand shaking wildly. If nothing else, I wanted one of them to bleed before they killed me. I hid it between my chest and Zane's back and waited.

Their engines died as they raked their snowmobiles sideways and nearly crashed into us before stopping. Baldy jumped off with the gun pointed.

"We meet again. Second and last time."

"Man, let's just go. No more. What about Jack?" asked Matt as he came up behind him.

"Jack doesn't know a thing. We'll say we tried to stop the terrible person who did this. Chased him the whole way, but we were too late." He took a step closer.

My hand hurt from squeezing the knife, but if I was going to do it, it had to be now. I gritted my teeth, turned, and drove the knife into his calf at the side. I squeezed my eyes shut, waiting for the gun to blow my head off.

The blast that came should have been the end. I expected to see... something. White light, my dad. I expected the noise to stop. Maybe even to feel my legs again if I could walk in heaven. But cold air nipped me, and the blast echoed into the hills.

I opened my eyes to see Baldy lying at my side, completely still. There was shouting, a car pulling up, but no pain. I didn't want to, but I leaned against Zane to lift up a few inches and look around. My mother stood on the ramp with a shotgun still shouldered. Her nightgown swirled around her bare feet, and she looked frozen like a statue in that position. I turned back. Matt knelt on the ground with his hands high. Tears streamed down his cheeks as Jim ran up behind him.

"I didn't mean to. I didn't mean to," Matt muttered, until the sirens drowned him out.

• • •

"I THOUGHT YOU weren't coming back," said Zane from the bedroom door. I hadn't seen him in two weeks. He still wore the bandage that started on his neck, covered part of his ear, and ended on his scalp. He'd bled a lot from the flesh wound, but he'd be fine.

I closed my book and smiled. "Mom decided we're keeping the place. We're coming back as much as I want."

He walked in closer and sat at the edge of the bed. "And how much is that?"

"Depends. There isn't much for me to do around here but eat Margie's gargantuan waffles at The Junction. Unless I had someone to take me snowmobiling."

"Wish I could, but sorry," he said standing.

"Oh. Yeah. I'm... sure you're busy." I stared at my book, trying to cover my disappointment. Of course he didn't want to. His babysitting job was over, and he'd almost been killed. Who would stick around after that? And why spend time with me when he could hit the slopes with a beautiful snow bunny who could ski?

Instead of walking away, he stepped to my left and picked up my hand. "I can't do it because Jim and I rigged Jack's snowmobile for you. Jack feels so bad. He wants you to have it. You're going to drive it yourself... next to me."

He stared at me, pulling my arm closer to his chest as he leaned over.

"I can't," I whispered as his face neared mine.

"Can't kiss me?"

"No, drive one myself."

"Marritt, you stabbed a guy. You can do anything."

Somehow I'd forgotten about stabbing Baldy, or Nicholas Baldwin, according to the police. That part had left my memory, blocking any notion that I'd had a part in saving us. But Zane was right, and I finally believed it.

I smiled and pulled the hand he held, closing the distance. Just before our lips met, I leaned over his shoulder and said, "Close your eyes, Larry. This is private."

MICHELE SHAW writes YA romantic suspense, short stories, and poetry with representation by Karen Grencik of Red Fox Literary. She eats way too much candy and has never met a dog she didn't love. You can find her on Twitter @veertothewrite or at her website: michelelshaw. com.

Third Place

Time Slime and Other Acne Cures

Wendy Sparrow

IT WAS A lot like being born—as he might have imagined it anyway. You fell out of a tube, naked, covered in goop, and wanting to cry. Only he was a sixteen year old with an IQ of 164 and early graduation in his future. Instead of crying, he stood up in the bright, white room, stared at the hazy vision of a man in military garb in front of him, and said, "Had you put a wind tunnel at the end of the tube I just came through, I'd be a lot cleaner." Reagan shook some of the goop from the end of his fingers. It was nasty and green, as if he'd just passed through some creature's nasal cavity.

"We tried that. Unless you'd also prefer to be hairless, this is preferable." The man with the name "Steel" on his badge gestured with a clipboard to a moving walkway. "If you'll just come over here," looking down at his clipboard, "Reagan Ronald Miller."

Reagan winced at hearing his middle name—his parents were big-time Republicans. He got on the walkway as directed. Just like in a ridiculous Hollywood film, the walkway ran him through a series of showers that thankfully rid him of the ooze that had covered his skin.

"Why are you doing this?" he asked as a blast of chemical-laced water beat at him from all sides.

The man walked along beside the enclosed cleansing station and flipped through the clipboard's papers. "Time slime. It'll give you burns on your skin if you don't get it washed off. It already burned off your clothes as you went through. Your skin will be next, and it's a lot of paperwork to requisition new skin."

If any of this had seemed more familiar and less fantastic, Reagan might have been having flashbacks of gym classes and miserable locker room moments from his less-than-ideal time spent at Seaside High. As it was, when he nearly flew off the end of the walkway after being gusted dry, he just thanked the man who handed him a robe to put on.

"That's it? Most people panic," the man said.

Reagan had found himself hurtling through a white tunnel of light at monumental speeds as his clothes burned off his body and his glasses ricocheted around him before shattering. One moment, he'd been standing at his high school locker; the next, he'd emerged from the tube, squelching out in a puddle of green, stringy goo. Still, when you were an outsider, a loner, and hyperintelligent to boot—you adapted. "Why should I? Other than the loss of my glasses—you've been perfectly reasonable."

The man snapped his fingers. "Right. You have that thing with your eyes. Something-sightedness. We don't have that anymore."

"Nearsightedness."

"Right." Steel sighed it out, as if already bored with the conversation. "Will you be able to see well enough for orientation?"

"I suppose so."

"Good. Follow me."

Reagan couldn't quite make out faces, but it looked as if he wasn't the only one clothed in a robe wandering the hallways of what appeared to be a spaceship. Several of the other people he passed were making more of a fuss than he was.

"How did I get here? Are you going to probe me again?" an old man yelled.

Steel chuckled at this and called over his shoulder, "It looks like you got stuck in 1984 again."

The military personnel near the old man muttered, "He seems to be the only one the computer grabs for all of Iowa no matter how we tweak the settings."

Reagan and his escort, Steel, a man in his twenties or thirties who had the build of a quarterback, went into a small room where a man in a lab coat sat in front of a large sheet of glass with glowing green lines, dots, and words on it. He was dragging things with his fingertips but turned to greet Reagan with a blurry, outstretched hand.

"Reagan Miller, it is an honor. I'm sorry we've inconvenienced you like this. We don't always get a choice, you see," the man in a lab coat said, standing and shaking Reagan's hand with enthusiasm. "The computer snatches the most intelligent or historically significant target closest to the time aberration's location and drags you here to central processing. You're both. It's an honor and a privilege, but mostly an honor."

Reagan's escort snorted. "Don't wet your pants, Bytes; just fill him in and let's get him back to his time and place."

"Bytes?" Reagan repeated.

"It's Carl Daniels," the lab coat guy said, and shook Reagan's hand again.

Reagan nodded, uncomfortable with the attention the guy was paying him. He almost preferred the detached boredom from Steel. "So, why am I here?"

"Right." Carl dropped onto a stool that seemed to have no legs or base and slid over to the pane of glass and circled a line that was pulsing in the center of a square. "This is the next four days of your life. Your relative location and time became infected with a time worm."

"A time worm?" Reagan asked.

"It's an unfortunate side effect of some stuff we did in the late twenty-third century; but as I can't argue with the results and it's job security for me, who am I to question?" Carl tapped the dot, and it pulsed and spit out a bunch of words. "Four days were shown to be the maximum amount of time that had no outer-reaching output shift. At four days, something significant happens that *must* happen. The worm will try to stop that—they're like that."

"They are?" Reagan asked.

"Yes. It infects someone around your time. It gets into the host's brain and sabotages a significant historical figure or the strongest culprit for change—so, you—it's coming for you. This sleeper parasite will attack suddenly and ruin your future if you don't administer the anti-venom to the host."

Reagan held up both his hands. "Whoa. My future? The strongest? It wouldn't be me it's after. I'm not the strongest anything." He flexed his arms. "See. Strong and my name have never been used in the same sentence."

Even with his hazy vision, he could see Carl blinking at him in confusion. "You're the most intelligent and inventive individual your age for miles and for decades. You're a genius. It's like you have no idea who you are."

Steel sighed and tapped on the paper on his clipboard. "He's from the nineteen nineties—the early nineteen nineties. The balance of power hadn't shifted. He's probably still viewed as weak among his peers."

"But he's the smartest."

"That would count against him back then. The computers are

muddled about who to grab in the nineties as the most logical victim for the worm. It was a strange time in the old planet's history. Everything was in flux. I'd still guess it's him, but I can see why he thinks he's puny and insignificant."

"I never said insignificant," Reagan said, but he'd been thinking it.

"Let's get on with this," Steel said. "You're slowing down my mission, and I'm due for a lunch break." He set aside the clipboard and took out an eight-inch metal rod with a glowing red tip and held it up to the back of Reagan's neck. "Hold still."

Reagan had frozen when the cold metal had met his skin, so he couldn't have moved if he wanted to. A moment later there was a pinch of pain that made him instinctively grab his neck.

"Ow."

"It's not that bad," Steel growled.

"You just shot something into my neck!"

"Yes, a time bomb that'll fry your memory at the end of the four days." He looked at his clipboard. "So, by Thursday, October 28, 1993, at sixteen hundred. That's as long as we could give you. A time blip indicates a significant event takes place just after that time."

Reagan rubbed frantically at his neck. "It's going to fry my memory?"

"Just your memory of these four days," Carl assured him. "You'll just think you've lost time."

"Well, that's reassuring." It wasn't reassuring.

"It's standard procedure. Now, Einstein, tell him what he needs to do to catch the worm."

"Do you even know who Einstein was?" Carl asked, sounding annoyed.

"Do you?" Steel asked.

"No," Carl admitted. "At least I knew who Reagan Miller was when he popped up on our roster."

"Big deal. You know the guy who invented time travel. Here, have a freaking medal."

"Wait. I invented time travel?"

They both froze.

"The beacon will fry this memory too, right?" Carl whispered.

"Yes," the other man whispered back.

"Yes, you did... in about forty years from your current age." Carl gestured at the board. "Now, time is linear, as you can see—until it gets messed up by time worms…which were not your fault, of course. You couldn't have predicted time worms in your day. The time worms will get into their host and take on most but not all of their mannerisms. Since it's in their brains, it'll know what they know and approximate their behavior. You simply need to go back to your time, find the time worm's host, and administer this." He held up a small, metal cylinder that he pressed into Reagan's hand. "It should be a walk in the park for one of the greatest minds of his time."

Reagan held the cylinder close to his eyes to see. It looked like a metal capsule meant to be swallowed like a pill. "I give it to them like a pill? They swallow it?"

"No, of course not," Steel said in disgust. "You shove it up their nose, and they'll fight you on it—believe it or not."

Of course he believed it. Anyone would fight having a metal cylinder shoved up their nose. In fact, if they didn't fight, he'd suspect they had something seriously wrong with them. "What if I can't find the host in four days—well, less than four days really?" It was a reasonable question and calling three and one *partial* day four days—didn't *make* it four days.

"Well, we come down from the sky in black helicopters, seal off the area, and run tests on everyone—just before we do a major memory wipe of everyone. We also have to go back and do this at the beginning of your four days." He held up four fingers and mouthed "four days."

It wasn't quite four days.

"Wow." Reagan stared at the pulsing green line that was the next three days or so of his life.

"Typically, we don't like to do that. We usually can trust that the person the computer chooses isn't a moron and can find someone acting strange if they're given four whole days."

"It's not quite four *whole* days," Reagan pointed out.

Steel raised his eyebrows and scribbled something on his clipboard. "Some people only get a day—and they do just fine."

"Although, it's very rare for a worm to choose such a populated setting—let alone a high school," Carl said.

"Everyone reinvents themselves every day in high school," Reagan said. "You can just start prepping the choppers."

Reagan didn't even interact with anyone if he could help it. He stayed focused on the goal: get through school—alive. Anything else he managed in high school was just bonus points really.

"Maybe we shouldn't tell anyone if Reagan Miller fails," Carl whispered. It was as if they thought he was deaf.

"No chance. There's a pool going with the guards. I've got a lot riding on him failing."

"What? You bet against Reagan Miller?"

Reagan stared at Carl, who seemed to believe in him like no one outside his parents ever had. *Reagan Miller* would have bet against Reagan Miller.

"So I just go back, find someone acting strange, and shove this thing up their nose?" Reagan asked, holding the cylinder aloft. "If I pick the wrong person, will it hurt them?"

Steel laughed in loud bursts before sobering and staring at him. "Wait? You were serious? Don't do that. Really. Don't. Also, remember, the worm will give the host no free will. They'll be willing to die trying to stop you." He took Reagan by the shoulders. "Don't get killed. We have to fill out all sorts of paperwork for that, and I'm up for a performance review soon." The guard nodded and hit Reagan's shoulder in a way that was meant to be comforting but only seemed to be comforting among jocks. Reagan just had a sore shoulder now. "There. Good. Ready?"

Was he ready? Were they joking? Okay. Time to man up and go save the world—from men in black helicopters. Reagan squared his shoulders. "Are you kidding? Danger is my mother's maiden name," he said. They didn't laugh. They should've laughed. "I guess I'm ready."

II

Three days, seven hours remaining

YOU KNOW THAT dream where you're naked in the middle of the halls at school and everyone points and laughs at you? It was like that— only during class time—so less pointing and laughing.

Amid shouts of "No, don't put me back where you found me!" Reagan was dropped in front of his locker, naked, but sans time slime because, apparently, that only happened when you went forward in time. An office aide, who really had her own issues, was the only witness to Reagan's quick grab of his backpack and dash out the nearest door into some bushes.

Reagan preferred to live by the motto " Be prepared," so he had clothes for after gym in his backpack. It was still going to cause nightmares for years to come, and he'd never be able to look that aide, Mrs. Henderson, in the eye for…well…ever. She'd probably need even more therapy for that moment that had thankfully been blurry for him. She already had enough kittens-dangling-on-ropes posters around her desk that students snickered at whenever they entered the office. Reagan would buy her another—it was only right. She'd have to "hang in there" and repress it like the rest of them.

Reagan dug his spare glasses out of his backpack.

It was good to be back in 1993 at the very least. When he picked up his backpack from the ground, something else caught his attention. No acne on his arms. While his zits weren't quite as severe on his arms, he'd still had some. He brushed a hand across his face. No, it was clear too. He lifted his shirt. None visible. Either the future society had gifted him with perfect skin or the time slime had somehow gotten rid of it. Maybe when he invented time travel, he'd make a note to bottle the time slime as an acne treatment.

He'd just slipped back into the school when someone grabbed his collar from behind and dragged him back against the lockers. His head slammed, dislodging his glasses, which he grabbed before his spares were lost too.

Even blurry, Josh didn't look happy. He was the younger, meaner version of Steel, the guard in the future. On the other hand, Josh had been slamming Reagan into lockers for years now, so there was some comfort in the repetition. Especially since it probably meant Josh wasn't his worm host, which was good—there'd be no way Reagan could wrestle Josh down to shove something up his nose.

It must have made him smile, because Josh growled, "Oh, you think that's funny, do you?"

"No." By now Reagan knew the answer to that question was always no.

Josh was in every sport the school had, and he'd bullied his way into popularity. The jean jacket he wore had been painstakingly inked with the school mascot—a shark—by a group of freshman girls who usually hung around him like a walking fan club.

"I'm telling you, stop drooling over my girlfriend."

"Your girlfriend?" Reagan repeated. The bell had just rung, and other students were milling through the hallways. Getting shoved into lockers had become such a regular occurrence, few even bothered to stop and watch.

"Lila. I know you've got a stupid little crush on her."

Normally, the rub of the lockers across his back would sting from aggravating his acne. Today, nothing. Huh.

"I've only spoken with Lila when she's asked me about math." Reagan might have the tiniest crush on her, but he wasn't aware it was *that* obvious *or* that Lila was Josh's girlfriend.

"Well, stop it."

"Stop helping her?"

"Josh?" a voice called from down the hall, and Lila herself was winding her way toward them. Josh immediately dropped Reagan, whose feet had been dangling an inch or two off the ground.

"Shut up about that," Josh muttered under his breath.

"What were you doing?" Lila asked as she made it to their sides. She was in the drama club and today wore a long sweatshirt with the word "Forsooth" scripted across it. She always wore leggings showcasing her thin, long legs. Her auburn hair was pulled back into a loose bun that had a pencil stuck in it to hold it in place. There was an ethereal other-worldly appeal to her slim body and pale looks—as if she could be an elf from Final Fantasy.

"Nothing," Josh said to her. "I can hold your books." He moved to take them from her, but she shifted slightly and shook her head. "Or not. I mean, that's cool."

Reagan bit back a smile. Josh was dealing with his own stupid little crush.

Lila turned to Reagan. "I have a test on Friday. Is there any chance we can get together and you can help me get ready for it?"

Reagan nodded but tried not to look too eager. First, he couldn't spend all his time with Lila or the black helicopters would be a given. Secondly, Lila was a hopeless cause. She was three inches taller than he and about fifty rungs higher on the social climb.

"But not at school. I don't want to meet at school," she said.

"The library?" They had study rooms there.

She smiled in a mysterious way. "No, not the library. I'll get back to you."

He just stared at her. This made no sense. None. At all.

Lila was nice to everyone—that was like her *thing*. Reagan had initially thought it was an act, but it had continued year after year when other girls grew out of their social conscience as it became less cool to care. Lila could be overly dramatic, but she was always nice. But wanting to spend time with him—even if it was studying—made no sense.

If she was infected with the worm, maybe it wasn't all bad. Maybe like the time slime it had its good aspects.

"Okay," Reagan said.

With a nod, Lila moved off down the hallway, gliding away on those long legs of hers. Josh and Reagan watched her go, probably with the same stupid look on their faces.

Yep, she probably had a time worm in her brain if she was eager to study math with him. Lila was the person he'd least enjoy stuffing a cylinder up her nose. It sucked really.

He ought to check out the rest of the student body and make sure, though. With any luck, he'd find someone else behaving more out of character. At the very least, he could push off tackling Lila and shoving the cylinder up her nose until the last possible second—like Thursday at 3:59 p.m.

Josh seemed to have lost his interest in pummeling him and just wandered off–Josh's attention span was about two nanoseconds.

Reagan walked slowly toward his class while eyeing the different social classes, watching for one of them to watch him back. Even if he wasn't much in the social hierarchy—in fact, he was in the lowest rank, right below the punk stoners who didn't much care for inclusion anyway—even then he was more likely to notice if anyone paid attention to him. Most days he felt invisible.

The hand that grabbed his shoulder startled him, making him jump. He'd been focusing so deeply he hadn't even noticed anyone around him.

He turned to see his friend Nick with his twin, Cody. Cody twitched, sniffed, and blinked behind the thickest glasses in the entire student body. Behind his back, most people called Cody "Twitch." They'd been born premature, with Nick being the sturdier of the twins. Even though they looked alike, with brown eyes and brown hair and a slight build, they weren't identical. Cody's twitchy behavior and hyperintrovert nature made him stand out—and among the geeky lower classes, that was something. Nick shifted in front of his twin as a group of jocks walked by. Nick even glared this time, which was unusual. Still, that's what they did: protect Cody. The entire nerd group united as a pack when it came to their weakest link, and no one was as sincere about this as Nick. Still, they'd all taken a beating or two intended for Cody. The world was cruel at times when it sensed weakness.

"Ask him," Cody said, with a nod at Reagan.

"Are we still doing Zelda after school?" Nick asked. "That new Korean kid, Erik, said he made it past that section of the Dark World."

"I think he's full of it," Cody said.

Nick nodded.

He should really try to solve this whole time worm thing. "I think maybe I'll stay and watch football practice." Weirder words had never dropped out of his mouth.

Cody laughed.

Nick narrowed his eyes.

Reagan didn't say anything. He couldn't explain. They'd just laugh at him. Plus, there was always the chance one of them had the worm, and he couldn't tip his hand.

Cody stopped laughing and blinked, his eyes hugely magnified behind his thick glasses. "Wait, you're serious?"

"Is this about Lila?" Nick asked.

"How would it be about Lila?" Reagan asked.

"Her play practice."

Oh, right. That might have made more sense than saying he was staying to watch football.

"Yeah," Reagan said. If he wandered around to the various after-school things, it wasn't a lie.

"You're really hung up on her," Cody said, taking a deep pull on his inhaler. Reagan moved to shield him from view. Not that there was anything wrong with Cody being asthmatic, but the pack was only as strong as its weakest link.

"Yeah." Reagan was—that wasn't a lie.

"Okay," Nick said in a tone implying the opposite.

"Great," Reagan said in the same tone.

Nick and Cody walked off, both giving him a look that indicated they thought *he* was the one with a worm in his head.

III

Two days, fours hours remaining

WELL, STAYING AFTER school the previous day had taught him less than nothing—other than facing jocks on their own turf just opened you to ridicule. He'd feared the same of beautiful drama girls, so he'd avoided the theater and had just gone home.

As he'd told them in the future, everyone reinvented themselves daily in high school. Half the kids had gone Goth today—what would they do tomorrow? Who knew? No one.

One of the girls in their group of nerds, Carrie, had taken advantage of the pancake-white face makeup look and literally coated her face in it. Combined with the black clothing she'd adopted, she looked like a mime running loose in the halls. Suddenly, Cody wasn't the weakest link anymore.

"So... ," Reagan said, sitting down at lunch across from Carrie. He gestured at her white face. He couldn't come up with anything else.

She was eating an apple and leaving trace amounts of her black lipstick on it. "What's with you? Are you using something new on your face?"

It took him a second to figure out she wasn't being sarcastic but was referring to his new, acne-free skin. Among their group, this wasn't a taboo subject.

"Yeah. Sort of."

The white makeup was hiding the bulk of her zits, but she might pay for that later with a backlash.

As much as he wanted to think this new Goth look was a sign that the worm was in Carrie and not in Lila after all, Carrie wasn't behaving so far out of character. Last week she'd been into grunge. At least with Goth she might bathe this week, and the black, ankle-length dress was better than last week's dirty flannel and Birkenstocks with socks.

"Are you going to the Halloween dance?" Carrie asked.

If it'd been someone else, he might have been concerned she was asking him. But Carrie was only theoretically interested in social inclusion and would be terrified at actually being thrown into a social environment.

He shrugged. You were allowed to dress up, and he had some

awesome costumes from when he'd been into Dungeons and Dragons.

Lila's perfume arrived before she did. That's not to say Lila wore heavy perfume. It was light and smelled sweet like cotton candy. He was just attuned to it because it belonged to Lila.

"Hey," Lila said, sitting down at the cafeteria table beside him.

He should just shove the cylinder up Lila's nose and get it over with. Across from him, Carrie's eyes widened in disbelief. Lila was sitting at the nerd's table. Silence had dropped across the entire cafeteria.

"I was thinking." Lila's auburn hair was down today, and she flipped it over her shoulder. Today's shirt was long and black and had a picture of the Eiffel Tower on it. "Maybe we could study at the Pebble Beach Café."

"You mean like a date?" Reagan blurted out.

Carrie's eyes, which had been impossibly wide before, nearly popped out.

Beside him, Lila shrugged.

"So, not a date?" Why was he still talking? Yesterday he'd found himself in the halls naked after traveling through time, yet that was more feasible than him going on a date with Lila.

This was Lila.

Lila shrugged again, getting up. "So, the Pebble Beach Café?"

"Sure."

Carrie was numbly shaking her head back and forth when Nick and Cody sat down.

"Erik did get us past that part in Zelda!" Cody announced.

"Reagan has a date with Lila!" Carrie announced.

The others from the group had arrived, and they stared at him with the same numb shock Reagan felt inside.

"So, no Zelda again today?" Cody asked.

"I guess not," Reagan said. He should really watch Lila more closely. It was only a matter of time before he'd be shoving a cylinder up her nose. Wouldn't that be fun?

The new Korean kid, Erik, sat down at the table. He smiled at all of them. "Did you hear about Zelda?"

Reagan sighed. When he *did* invent time travel, he might come back to these four days and make it a do-over. This sucked.

IV

One day, one hour remaining

LILA WAS BRILLIANT in *The Merchant of Venice*. It was almost worth sitting in the dark back seats of the theater to watch her practice. He was more certain than ever she was the host infected with a worm. She was too brilliant to even want to study with him. He was like time slime in her social orbit.

Since it was a dress rehearsal, Lila was dressed in Portia's costume. It was the first time he'd seen her in anything other than an oversize shirt and leggings. He'd felt she was out of his league then. It was nothing to how he felt seeing her in an Elizabethan-era costume. It more than emphasized how far she was above his reach. The fact that she'd spoken to him—rather than just passing him a note or calling him at home—said it was definitely the worm's influence.

The back door of the theater opened, casting a rectangle of light across the darkened theater. The door's slam brought everyone's attention to the back. Reagan had ducked down when he'd seen the outline of the person entering. Few students were as big and imposing as Josh.

"Lila!" Josh shouted, interrupting the players on the stage—as if it was his right.

From his position crouched on the floor, Reagan could hear grumblings from the students at the front of the theater. Lila's heavy dress swished and snapped as she made her way down the aisle to where Josh had stopped in the back—just a row up from Reagan's hiding place.

"What is it, Josh? Can't you see that I'm busy?"

"Let's go out. Tonight. After you're done with this." This method of ordering people around may have worked in the past for Josh; but Reagan got the sense from Lila's sigh that, worm or not, she wasn't keen on being ordered around.

"It's a school night."

Josh snorted a laugh.

"I'm serious," Lila said. "I told my parents I wouldn't let the play mess with my grades, and I'm worried about failing math."

Josh snorted again. "That's why you've been talking with that geek?"

There was a shrug in her voice as she said, "I like Reagan. He's nice.

He doesn't talk down to me. He doesn't talk down to anyone."

"Why would he talk down to you? He's nothing, Lila."

Just what Reagan was thinking.

"He's not. He's smart and sweet."

That would be the worm talking. Though, once again, it was confusing as to whether this worm was as detrimental as those guys from the future had made it sound. The worm might be his only chance to get a date during high school.

"Well, whatever. Go to the dance with me then."

Lila sighed. "I'm already planning on going with someone else."

"Who?" Josh sputtered out.

"None of your business. Now leave. I have to get back to the play."

"What?"

The swish and snap of the heavy tapestry fabric indicated Lila had said all she was going to on the subject.

Josh stormed through the back door. It slammed against the outer wall with a vengeance.

It was much quieter when Reagan snuck through the same door a few minutes later.

Out in the hall, Cody and Nick were waiting, leaning against a nearby wall.

"What are you doing here?" Reagan asked, surprised. It wasn't like them to hang around this place after school let out. They'd all garnered too much abuse when it was actually in session for them to hang around after. "Wait, was there chess club today?"

Cody shook his head quickly before taking out his inhaler and breathing in a puff. He pointed at Nick.

Nick frowned at Reagan. "I think you're making a mistake. This whole thing with Lila—it's a mistake."

Yeah, it was. If not for the worm, Lila never would have even noticed him.

Reagan shrugged—he was beginning to see how useful this shrugging thing was. Lila had perfected it, of course, and he'd only be able to use it among his friends; but it was still nice for getting out of awkward conversations.

"You're being stupid," Nick said.

Once again the shrug, because Reagan really couldn't argue with Nick's opinion. Hopefully, Lila's memory of this time would be erased too.

"I don't think he's going to listen to you," Cody puffed out with punctuating breaths.

Nick threw his hands up in the air and stalked off, with Cody following along behind him.

Reagan watched them go, promising himself that next week he'd spend every day playing Legend of Zelda instead of spying on his fellow students. The nice thing about being the bottom of the totem pole is that they tended to forgive one another fairly easily.

The door opened behind him, and he turned to see Lila in the theater door.

"Oh, hey, that was you. I thought so. We're still on for tomorrow, right?" she asked.

"You knew I was there?"

She grinned. It was definitely the worm.

He nodded. Perhaps too vigorously. "Yeah, sure, tomorrow." It was a good thing that bomb thing was going to fry his memory. This would be an awkward moment he'd obsess over later otherwise. Not that it could match the moment when he shoved a cylinder up Lila's perfect nostril, but it would be close.

Lila waved and went back into the theater.

She'd known. Did that mean she'd known he was there when she'd been talking to Josh? Maybe.

It was unreal.

He went home and wrote up everything he'd seen and heard and suspected about time travel. This was probably against the rules, and it was doubtful his future self would believe it; but it was worth a try.

It sounded as if he had a date with Lila. Even with a time worm involved, there were even more impossible things in play than time travel.

V

Twenty-five minutes remaining

REAGAN PULLED UP to the café and took a deep breath, rolling the cylinder between his fingers before pocketing it. He couldn't believe he was about to shove something up Lila's nose. He wasn't completely certain the black helicopters were a worse scenario at this point.

With another heartfelt sigh, he climbed out of his red Chevy Sprint just as a white Geo Metro pulled up alongside him.

"I can't let you do this," Nick said, getting out.

Cody got out, looking uncomfortable.

"I'm just here to tutor Lila," Reagan said, holding up an algebra book.

"That's not why you're here, and you know it," Nick said. He came around to stand in front of Reagan's path.

Reagan rolled his eyes. Even if Nick was right, it wasn't like him to try and stop Reagan from doing something stupid. If Reagan was Cody, that would be different; but in general, they let each other screw up and just made a show of solidarity afterward.

Actually, it *really* wasn't like Nick.

Reagan spun toward Cody and shoved him against the car.

Cody blinked up at Reagan in confusion. "Hey, why'd you do that? I told you he'd be pissed, Nick!"

Nick stood still, blocking Reagan's path. He hadn't moved to protect his twin.

Reagan pulled Cody back on his feet. "Sorry, this is going to sound crazy, but your brother has a worm controlling his brain."

"Like in *Wrath of Khan*?" Cody asked.

"Exactly!" Reagan said, glad for an easy explanation.

Cody looked back and forth between Nick and Reagan. Nick didn't move or deny the accusation. He just stood there. Finally, Cody nodded. "He's been acting strange for a week now. I thought he was sick or something. You should have seen how lousy he's been on Zelda."

Reagan wanted to slap his hand against his forehead. He could have figured this out days ago. He was such an idiot. He pulled the cylinder from his pocket. "I need to shove this up in his nose. It'll get rid of the worm."

"Okay, I'll hold him down."

They advanced on Nick, who reacted by narrowing his eyes and crossing his arms. Between the two of them, they were able to tackle him and pull him behind the café. Cody lost his glasses and got elbowed in the process, but he'd insisted he be the one to sit on Nick's chest and pin him down.

Shoving something up someone's nose is not an experience Reagan ever wanted to repeat. Even as he was doing it, he kept reminding himself it could have been worse—it might have been Lila.

As soon as the pill-sized cylinder was no longer visible, Nick's eyes rolled back in his head. A moment later he sneezed out the cylinder with a groan. The cylinder ricocheted off Cody's chest and pinged into the side of a nearby Dumpster.

"Do you think it worked?" Cody whispered, rubbing his head where he'd taken Nick's elbow. Cody had proven to be much stronger than he looked. It was as if he was in his element.

"I don't know," Reagan admitted.

Nick just lay there. Finally, his eyelids flickered open, and he stared up at Cody.

"Why are you sitting on my chest?" Nick asked. "And where are your glasses? You know Mom will kill both of us if you lost them."

Laughing, Cody got up. Cody looked better than Reagan had ever seen him look. He wasn't even wheezing from the physical exertion of pinning Nick—and Nick hadn't gone down without a fight. Reagan could feel bruises forming from all the kicking and punching.

"Aren't you supposed to be on a date?" Cody asked.

"Whoa! Reagan has a date?" Nick asked.

Waving over his shoulder, Reagan bolted into the café—late.

VI

Two minutes remaining

HE SLID INTO the booth across from her. She'd brightened when he'd walked in. None of this made sense. If she didn't have a worm infecting her…

Could there be two worms?

"I thought maybe you'd changed your mind," she said.

Reagan held up the math book. "I told you I'd help you study." He wouldn't ever back out on a thing like that.

Lila stared at the book he'd set on the table between them. "You really thought we were studying?" Her nose wrinkled up before she smiled. "That's so… sweet."

"Really? What *are* we doing here?"

He could swear she blushed. Her skin was really pale, but he could swear she was embarrassed.

"I like you, Reagan. I like you a lot. You're sweet and cute and…I like you. It's a date."

That was it. There'd been two worms. Maybe the cylinder could be used twice. Maybe he could retrieve it and disinfect it or something. A girl like Lila didn't deserve having a cylinder shoved up her nose, let alone a used one. He glanced down at his calculator watch just as a blinding pain exploded across the back of his head, and everything went black.

VII

REAGAN OPENED HIS eyes. He was in that café near the beach—with Lila. What on earth had just happened? Last thing he remembered, he was at school in front of his locker.

"Are you okay?" Lila asked, staring at him in concern.

"I'm fine. I think." He glanced down at his watch. Whoa. He'd just lost time. Days even. Maybe he'd had a migraine or something. His head felt like an explosion had just occurred inside it. He rubbed a hand against his neck at the base of his skull where it felt swollen and warm. He swore he smelled something burning too. Burned hair. Burned brain. Something. "I think something just blew my mind."

Lila laughed, reached across, and put her hand on his on the table. "That's what I like about you, Reagan. You're so funny and nice."

Reagan just stared at their hands—together. What was going on?

A knock on the window beside him drew their attention. Cody was on the other side of the glass with his twin brother—looking as disoriented as Reagan felt. Cody held up a small metal cylinder and gave Reagan a thumbs-up with a grin. A moment later, Cody dragged his brother out of view.

"Cody's nice. He's in my English class," Lila said, still with her hand on his.

This was all so strange. She was practically holding his hand.

Lila cleared her throat. "So, I was wondering if you were going to the dance?"

"The dance?"

"Yes."

"Uhh." He had no idea where she was going with this or what alternate dimension he'd stepped into.

"I think we should go together."

"Together?"

She laughed. "Are you just going to repeat everything I say?"

"Uhh."

She leaned forward, meeting his eyes. "Lila, I'd love to go to the dance with you," she said slowly.

"Okay."

It wasn't brilliant. It wasn't even what she'd intended; but it made her laugh, and he loved her laugh. Maybe he even loved her… a little… it was hard to say. After all, he wasn't even sure what he was doing, let alone how he felt.

Someone put a quarter into the jukebox, and "Can't Help Falling in Love" by UB40 started playing.

"I love this song. It's timeless," Lila said with a sigh. "I should put it on a mix tape."

She was still holding his hand.

"You should come sit next to me," she said.

He did, and that's when he noticed the math book. "So, are we studying?"

Lila pulled his arm across her shoulders when he settled beside her. Whoa. What was going on? Maybe his friends would be able to fill in some of these missing blanks later.

"No, we're on a date."

"We're on a date?"

"Lila, you're cool, and I think you're beautiful," she said.

Reagan smiled. He wasn't an idiot. He was a genius, in fact. "Lila, you're cool, and I think you're beautiful." Whatever had gotten him here to this moment with Lila, he was pretty darn happy to be here.

It was awesome, in fact.

Very awesome.

"I was thinking maybe we'd go to the Halloween dance as Zelda and Link." Lila leaned into his side with a sigh.

"You like Legend of Zelda?"

"I love it, but no one in drama does. I've been trying to work up the nerve to invite myself to the parties I always hear you and your friends talking about at lunch."

She'd been eavesdropping on their lunch table?

"They're not really parties."

She shrugged.

His arm hurt a little from being around her shoulders with their disparate heights, and this was probably the weirdest and scariest thing he'd ever done, but some things were just worth it.

Very worth it.

And maybe it was about time.

WENDY SPARROW: At home in the Pacific Northwest, Wendy writes for both an adult and young adult crowd. She has two wonderfully quirky kids, a supportive husband, and a perpetually messy house because writing is more fun than cleaning. She cherishes ellipses, survives on Mountain Dew, and believes every story needs a happily-ever-after. Most days she can be found on Twitter at @WendySparrow, where she'll talk to anyone who talks back and occasionally just to herself. She took second place in last year's *Mystery Times Ten*.

The Shame of West Landry

KC Sprayberry

FLAMES SHOT THROUGH the roof of the abandoned, historic Mars Theater on the edge of West Landry, Georgia. A roar and crackle drove back the men, women, and children on the corner of the street between the theater and the railroad tracks. Murmurs of disgust raged from them. Bree Sandowski tried to block out the anger as she watched yet another building burning during this too-hot summer.

"When will this stop?" Bree thought. "What will it take? Another murder?"

Week after week during record-breaking heat, houses and businesses burned. No one in the police department showed the least interest in stopping the arsonist, even though more than a dozen people had perished in the flames. It was like the winter Bree's parents died in an explosion. Who would have thought the second story of the old glove factory would have crushed their car? It was also like the summer of '65 when her great-uncle came back from Vietnam with a haunted expression and then disappeared when the historic West Landry Grocery burned down.

"This isn't coincidence," Bree thought. "It can't be." She nibbled on her lower lip as her mind took a direction she didn't like. "But it can't be the same person. Can it?"

She lost herself in thought about how an arsonist could have been around from 1965 till now, almost fifty years later. The idea sounded so outrageous that she almost discarded it without wasting any more time. For Bree was a very special person, with special abilities. She'd recently celebrated her eighteenth birthday and had no one in the world except Nana Emily. But Nana Emily was lost in the fog of Alzheimer's and would never live in West Landry again. Nana was now a resident of an assisted-living center and most days didn't even recognize her only grandchild.

"I really should visit Nana," Bree thought. "I might be able to get her to tell me something about the summer Great-Uncle Jack disappeared."

The raging fire mesmerized Bree, even more so when a long line of ghosts stood in a wavering line between the spectators and the police tape blocking off the street. Those ghosts looked from Bree to the fire and back.

"I know, I know," she thought at the spirits. "But I can't do anything right now."

The ghosts glared at her and then turned their backs. As well they should. Bree felt shame every time she encountered one of the spirits. She was gifted with a talent that allowed her to communicate with those who had died as a result of a violent act. Every single phantasm now occupying the area between the fire and the crowd had perished in the many unsolved blazes that had left West Landry looking like a war zone.

A thin wail rose from the Mars Theater, an appeal for help that went unnoticed by others. Bree concentrated on the building. Flames still shot out of the roof and reached for the sky, but the lower floor was untouched. This was the most unusual fire she'd ever witnessed. Firefighters aimed their hoses at the flames, but nothing stopped the red and yellow fingers of destruction from reaching for the buildings on either side.

"It's the Shame of West Landry," a man yelled. "Listen to me, those of you who live here, listen well. Someone died this day, and still none of you will speak up with what you know."

Bree searched the crowd for the speaker's position but saw no one standing alone as others backed away in fear. Only she stood out, as different from the others as night was from day. Her pale, creamy complexion produced freckles if she stood in the sun for very long, and her bright blond hair was a cap of curls around a heart-shaped face. On this impossibly hot day, she wore a pair of worn-out sneakers, cut-off jeans shorts, and a tank top, far different attire from the slacks and dress shirts on the men and dresses on the women.

None of the people approached Bree, and she wondered why. All of those here counted themselves as ancestors of the more than fifteen hundred slaves who had made up Wallis County before the Civil War freed them. Thirty African Americans from that time were freed by their owner, all one family, one Bree knew well.

"Oh, baby girl," a familiar voice said. "It's so bad. So bad. I just cain't believe it's come to this."

A work-roughened hand touched Bree's shoulder, and she resigned herself to being treated as a small child incapable of doing anything but getting into messes. No matter what the age, the residents of West Landry, be they younger than she or old enough to remember the troubled times of the 1950s and 1960s, called her baby girl. She was their special child, gifted with a talent to speak with those they'd lost and the only Anglo who dared to live in the least-appreciated area of Landry, Georgia.

"Hello, Miz Mazie," Bree said. "It's bad but nothing we can't handle."

She left unsaid that this fire would probably end up like all the rest: unsolved. Bree's attention wandered when Kevin Jacobs, a firefighter and the man who held her interest, jerked a runaway hose from the ground and aimed the spray at the smoldering sides of the pawn shop south of the theater. A tall man, well over six feet, towering above Bree's diminutive five feet four inches, his deep black hair plastered against the sides of his face exposed through the mask of his helmet. His strong arms guided the hose back and forth as he fought to save the pawn shop while another group of firefighters climbed a ladder to work the roof and second floor of the Mars Theater.

"It's real bad, baby girl," Miz Mazie said with a hitch in her voice. "My brother, old Joe Jackson himself, called me last night. He's a comin' home, baby girl. He was supposed to be here hours ago, but I haven't heard a word from him since last night."

Hearing Joe Jackson was coming back to West Landry gave Bree hope that she might find her Great-Uncle Jack. Jack Sandowski and Joe Jackson disappeared the night the first fire started during the summer of '65. The police, led by Zachariah Sandowski, Bree's great-uncle three times removed, accused the men of arson and attempted murder, claiming they skipped town to avoid going to prison. Bree knew, from the stories her nana had told her, that the truth was far from Zachariah's accusations but had no hard evidence to prove what most knew.

Zachariah was now the police chief, and his son, Benjamin, headed the detective division of the Landry Police Department. Benjamin was like a clone of his father. Bree avoided both of them as much as she could. There was another Sandowski relative she could also do without seeing. Logan was the same age as Bree but her exact opposite. She saw Logan skulking near the police tape and wondered why he was in West

Landry. He never came around unless there was something he wanted.

Bree reluctantly tore her attention from the fire to concentrate on Miz Mazie. The elderly woman was as dark as midnight without a moon, with expressive brown eyes. Her lower lip trembled, and she tightened her grip on Bree's shoulder.

"I done tried," Miz Mazie confided. "But Joe's cell phone, it goes straight to that fancy voice mail. I must have left near about three dozen messages in the last couple of hours, but Joe hasn't called back." She flicked her gaze to the fire. "And now this. I just know something awful has happened to Joe."

Two other people shared Bree's talent: Nana Emily and Miz Mazie. Bree had learned how to deal with ghosts from those women but had long since surpassed their teachings. Neither had offered much advice since Bree had entered fifth grade, and she hoped that trend would end today for Miz Mazie.

"What makes you think something awful has happened to Joe?" Bree asked.

"It's here." Miz Mazie removed her hand from Bree's shoulder to touch the spot over her heart. "I know my older brother came up against no good."

"Bree!" Logan shouted, and elbowed his way through the crowd. "Outta my way, niggers!"

His slur caused Bree to walk away from Miz Mazie without a word and stride through the now-angry crowd to confront her cousin. Logan snarled again at those in his way and used the n word.

"Don't you dare use that word again," Bree snapped. "How dare you, Logan Sandowski?"

"Everyone knows how lazy these folks are." Logan stopped in front of Bree.

She stared in shock at his arms, exposed by the wife-beater shirt he wore. Logan had a weak chin and blond hair a bit darker than hers. His hazel eyes looked her up and down as an appreciative grin crossed his face.

Bree ignored the insulting look that usually angered her and focused on the skin on Logan's arms. It was red. Not the red from spending too much time in the sun but the red that looked as if he'd been burned, maybe a flash burn.

"What happened to you?" Bree asked, and almost choked when he moved closer.

He reeked of gasoline. Bree cast a glance at the fire, thought about how it had almost exploded on the top floor but not the bottom floor, and put together all the other fires in West Landry this summer with Logan's visits.

What have you done, Logan? Bree thought before she asked, "Why are you down here? Won't your mama have a hissy fit if she hears about you hanging around West Landry?"

It wasn't Bree's intention to drive Logan away but rather to entice him to stay. She hoped her snide comment did the trick. Logan almost never did what his mama wanted.

"Got business down here." Logan swept a casual hand toward the Mars Theater. "See, Mama and Daddy bought that old place for me last week. So it's mine, and I want to know who burned it up." He gave Bree a knowing smile. "I planned to fix the place up, even make sure the Negro Balcony could be used again."

At least he'd not said the n word. Bree breathed a sigh of relief at that. She suspected, though, that Logan had no such plans for fixing up the old building. He hated anything not produced in the last five years and thought history was for idiots who couldn't handle the present.

"Get back!" Kevin's voice rang out over the noise of the fire and grumblings from the crowd as Logan stepped on a few feet while leaving Bree in an open spot among the spectators. "Move back, the roof's collapsing."

Seconds later, as a firefighter burst from the theater, the smoke parted. Bree gasped along with everyone else when a flame-ravaged body tumbled out from under the stairs and flopped onto the floor. It was hard to tell from here, but Bree had her suspicions as to the identity of the person.

"There's a body!" the firefighter who'd just dived out of the building hollered. "Damn! There's a body in there. I almost tripped over it."

Everyone moved closer to the police tape for a better look at the body sprawled on the floor of the old theater. Speculative whispers echoed around the street. Logan glanced at the building, and his face paled. He began to back away.

"Will you tell this time, West Landry?" A strange voice boomed in Bree's ears, and she stared in amazement as a new spirit formed in front of the theater.

This was a tall man, well muscled, and wearing very old camouflage fatigues. A black beret folded under his shoulder tab puzzled her until she saw three more spirits moving out from under the stairs.

"Speak up, West Landry," another male voice said, coming from a spirit who wore a duplicate of the first one's uniform. "Tell the truth. How many more have to die?"

One of the speakers was African American and the other Anglo. They stood side by side, shoulders touching. Bree had the sense they were buddies, more than comrades in arms, closer than brothers. The other two ghosts wore slacks and shirts. One was a man and the other a woman. Both were replicas of the pictures on Nana Emily's bedside table at the assisted-living center. The two men in uniform were in another picture. Bree was staring at the ghostly forms of her parents, her great-uncle, Jack and his closest friend, Joe Jackson.

"Oh no!" Bree thought, and smothered a shocked gasp. "Poor Miz Mazie. This will come close to destroying her."

"Joe!" Miz Mazie howled in grief-stricken tones. "Oh, my brother, Joe. What have they done to you?"

"Tell the world, Sister," the first spirit cried, confirming Bree's suspicions about his identity. "It started the night I went missing. Me and Jack, the two of us knew too much. He didn't make it out of West Landry that night but I did, and then I made the mistake of coming back to this town."

Those watching the fire began to wander away. Their downcast faces told Bree the ghost didn't need her to remind her neighbors of their shame.

"Tis your shame, West Landry," Joe Jackson yelled in a deep baritone that rang out in the suddenly quiet street. "You hang your heads and walk away. Look at them." He flung a misty, black hand at the ghosts gazing upon the other spirits guarding the Mars Theater as the fire died down. "These are your people, and you let them wait to pass through the pearly gates because you're cowards."

The word *cowards* rang through the crowd. A few of the men muttered about saving the living; but most, especially the women, appeared as if they felt it was time to reveal what was only spoken of in whispers, and then only when they were certain no one would reveal what the poorest section of Landry knew.

"They can't say anything now," Bree thought, and looked around for Logan. "Please, don't let any of them say the words."

She finally located her cousin slouched in the leather seat of his candy-apple-red Mustang. With a roar of eight cylinders revving up, Logan drove away. Bree watched him leave but knew he'd be back. He always came back after the fire trucks left.

"Do your duty, West Landry," another spirit spoke up, taking Bree back to the faint memories she had of her parents. It was her dad.

She moved closer to the police tape but stopped when Zachariah and Benjamin glanced in her direction. The four ghosts focused on Bree and smiled. Their teeth gleamed in the sun as if they were real instead of bits of mist.

"Emily knows what we all know," Great-Uncle Jack said to Bree. "Make Emily tell you what she knows."

The sadness running through Bree felt almost as bad as the moments after the doctor pronounced Nana Emily unfit to live at home any longer. Bree turned away from the ghosts and moved back to Miz Mazie. The elderly woman stood in the center of a circle of neighbors, all of them clucking and attempting to comfort her.

"Did Nana Emily tell you about what they said?" Bree jerked her head at the ghosts. "Is there a way to find that information?"

"Don't do this, baby girl." Tears traveled from Miz Mazie's eyes through the wrinkles on her face. "Oh, baby girl, don't let them men hurt you too."

Long-held suspicion blamed the Sandowski men, Zachariah and Benjamin, and more recently Logan for the fires. Many of the grandfathers in West Landry said Zachariah had a fascination with fires from the time he could walk. Benjamin was caught lighting a fire in a trash can when he was in his early teens. And Logan, he was the worst of the lot. Bree knew for a fact that Logan had caused the fire at the old high school in West Landry six months ago, but there was no proof just her word against his. She couldn't accuse a cop's son and the police chief's grandson of arson without physical proof.

"I can't let this keep happening, Miz Mazie," Bree said, and indicated the ghosts. "They deserve a rest. Do you want someone else to join them?"

"No." Miz Mazie shook her head. "But I don't want to lose you either, baby girl. Please, don't get involved. Let someone else do it."

"There is no one else." Bree turned back to the fire and waved at Kevin.

"Hey, Bree." Kevin loped over to the tape and grinned at her.

That grin made him look as if he was still an all elbows-and-knees ninth grader at Landry High School. Bree returned the grin and leaned close.

"Joe Jackson is the body inside the building," Bree whispered, after making sure Zachariah and Benjamin were nowhere close. "I'm going to solve this mystery finally. Joe was on his way back to reveal what happened almost fifty years ago, but now he can't unless I do something."

"Wait until tonight." Kevin frowned. "I'm off duty then and can help." He glanced at where the Sandowski cops spoke in low tones. "Don't do anything that might attract Zachariah's or Benjamin's attention."

"Not you too," Bree said in disgust. "It has to end, Kevin. Look at Miz Mazie." She flung a hand in the direction of the grieving woman. "We have to stop this before anyone else dies."

Kevin returned to the fire without acknowledging how right Bree was. She waited for Miz Mazie to go home and then sidled close to another woman, Esther Johnson. Esther was the source of news in West Landry, unless she decided she didn't want to talk about events that hurt her folks. So far Bree had failed to entice Esther into revealing what she knew about the fires.

"It has to stop, Miz Esther," Bree said. "You know something. Otherwise you'd have been talking about this summer's fires on every street corner."

"Ain't talkin', baby girl." Miz Esther turned her back. "Won't let no one call me a gabby old woman agin. It's gettin' downright painful hearin' all them menfolk say I'm good for nuthin' but makin' trouble."

She was right about that. But the men in West Landry only spoke harshly of her habit of repeating whatever she saw—with a few embellishments—to stop her from getting hurt like others who'd accused the Sandowskis of criminal acts.

"If you don't talk, someone else will die, Miz Esther," Bree said.

"Please, tell me what you saw last week. I know you were outside that house that burned. I saw you hurrying home."

Miz Esther had not only hurried home after the house down the street from Bree's had burst into flames, she denied having been on the street at all. All those who'd seen her shuffling past in her flapping, faded red house shoes with her hands over her eyes knew differently.

"You saw who set that fire last month, Miz Esther," Bree said in a low tone. "You know it and I know it. Why else would you run down the street with your hands over your eyes? You might have tripped and broken your hip again."

Miz Esther gave Bree a look of eternal shame. She nodded and glanced around, her gaze settling on Zachariah and Benjamin.

"Them men, they were there; but they didn't set the fire," Miz Esther said. "It were–"

"Hush your mouth, old woman," a teenage girl shouted. "Just hush your mouth. We don't need no trouble down here. And you know they'll cause trouble."

Bree turned toward the teenager, a girl she'd graduated with back in May, and opened her mouth. The girl raced away.

"You won't run away from this, Shelly!" Bree shouted. "No one can run away from this anymore. Help us make West Landry safe."

Benjamin walked toward Bree, but she held on to Miz Esther's elbow and guided the elderly woman around the corner, through the Goodwill parking lot, and back down West Main Street to where they both lived. Bree had a moment's panic when she heard the engine of Logan's car but didn't stop moving until they stood on Miz Esther's front porch.

"Who set that fire last month?" Bree asked. "Tell me and I can help."

"Gotta get away from here," Miz Esther said, and looked around. "Gotta go visit my sister up Soddy Daisy way. She'll help me hide until them men forget I saw Logan soakin' that house in gasoline and lighting it with a match."

She dashed into her house. The door banged shut, and the sound of a lock turning prevented Bree from asking more. Bree walked down the steps of the rickety porch and out to the sidewalk. Across the street was the house where she lived, a well-maintained Antebellum home out of keeping with the ramshackle buildings that surrounded it.

"I need more." Bree looked around for any sign of Logan, but he was nowhere in sight. "But how?"

All the fires in West Landry since the first one almost fifty years ago had been declared arson. Zachariah and Benjamin had always vowed to find the person or people responsible, even going so far as to put out wanted alerts for Joe Jackson and Jack Sandowski. Bree had never believed her great-uncle and Miz Mazie's brother were guilty of anything but being in the wrong place at the wrong time. Miz Esther's statement was a beginning, but Bree needed more.

The ghosts from the fire appeared in the middle of West Main Street. A few cars drove through the crowd of spirits but none left, nor did they stop staring at Bree and whispering for her to do something.

"This is so hard," Bree thought. "I've never been able to help all these ghosts, and now they want me to figure out the mystery in a couple of hours. I really need to talk to Nana Emily."

Talking to Nana Emily would do nothing but frustrate Bree. Her nana hadn't said a sensible word in ages. All Nana talked about was a burglary at their home a couple of months ago.

"No," Bree whispered, and started across the street, striding through the many ghosts in her path. "Nana talked about how wrong it was. The burglary." She stopped and stared at her open front door. "What? Who?"

She crept up onto the porch and paused at the door to listen for any sign of an intruder. Bree knew she should call the cops but also feared her cousins would show up. That was what happened the night of the burglary, which occurred while Bree and Nana Emily were at church. The report Benjamin took indicated nothing of importance was taken and minimal damage done, if one could call the destruction of the precious knickknacks Nana had collected all her life minimal. He left after laughing off Bree's and Nana's concerns.

"No one would bother with this place," Benjamin had said. "There's nothing worth stealing in this dump."

He'd walked out and slammed the door behind him, causing a porcelain kitten playing with a ball of yard to tumble from a shelf near the entry hall. The crash had disturbed Nana Emily more than Benjamin's dismissal of the burglary. She'd hurried over to the door to lock it and then gone into her study and locked that door. No amount of pleading on Bree's part had convinced Nana to come out.

"Why would the burglar return?" Bree asked. "It's not anyone from

West Landry." She glanced up and down the street. "Where is everyone?"

At this time of day in the summer, it wasn't unusual for children to run around on the street, play pickup games of baseball, or ride their bikes. Today there was no one in sight. The houses all had a shuttered look to them, with curtains or blinds drawn over their windows and doors tightly closed. Not a sound came from the other residents or from inside Bree's house.

"I hope the house is empty," Bree said as she went inside.

No one popped out from one of the many empty rooms or dashed down the stairs as she entered. Bree stared in shocked amazement at the litter on the floor. Stuffing from the antique sofa floated in the air and made her sneeze violently for a couple of minutes. The equally old table beside the door was now nothing but splinters on the floor. Pictures that had hung on the walls were tossed everywhere, the glass in the frames shattered. She picked her way through the mess and glanced in all directions, taking in the destruction.

"How will I ever figure out what's missing?" she asked.

This was far worse than the first burglary. Bree leaned over to pick up two pictures: the one of her parents, the other of Great-Uncle Jack with Joe Jackson when they were in Vietnam. Whoever had broken in had used a knife to slit the pictures across the faces. Sorrow raced through Bree. As far as she knew, there was no negative, nor had Nana Emily ever gotten around to letting Bree scan these pictures into her computer. A part of Bree's past—a very important part—had been destroyed.

"This is personal," she whispered. "And that means Logan."

Yet, she still had no hard proof or any way of involving the police. Even asking the sheriff to intervene wouldn't work. Zachariah would say that Bree was acting like a hysterical female, and the sheriff would ignore her request, if she made one.

"You won't stop me, Logan," Bree vowed. "But did you find what you were looking for?"

The sound of Logan's car drifted through a window to her left. Bree glanced in that direction and discovered her cousin had gone so far as to smash out the century-old leaded glass. Even the window frame hadn't escaped destruction, with deep gouges in the wood.

"What do you want, Logan?" Bree asked. "Why is it so important?"

She went over the events of the night of the first burglary, but nothing much had happened in West Landry that day. The only thing Bree could come up with was a small fire a couple of days before. But that fire was nothing like any of the others plaguing West Landry. An empty lot overgrown with stunted pine trees and grass had burned late one night. The fire chief had said it wasn't arson and had probably been caused when someone threw a cigarette out the window of their car.

"What if it wasn't a cigarette?" Bree wondered. "What if Nana saw something that night." She looked into Nana's study, the one room Bree had avoided entering since putting her nana into assisted living. "Nana Emily kept all her important stuff in there." She hesitated to enter the room. "But I really don't want to go through it. That would be so weird."

Weird or not, Bree's intuition screamed that the answer to the burglaries and fires lay in Nana's study. Bree stepped over the broken and shattered possessions she'd come to think of as an important part of her life. She walked into the study and laid the destroyed photographs on Nana's desk.

"It's in here somewhere," Bree thought. "But where?"

The rolltop of the desk was askew in its track, and she tried to raise it fully; but the slats refused to move. Bree reached up under the top and felt around. The drawers were out and blocking movement. Smiling, she pushed the drawers back into place—all but one that refused to move.

"Hope this works." Bree shoved upward on the desktop, rising on her toes as it moved this time.

"My little girl, all grown up," a female voice said. "Look for Emily's box, Bree. Oh, my little Sabrina, I wish we were with you to help figure this out."

"Thanks, Mom." Bree looked over her shoulder and found four ghosts in the room with her.

Her parents smiled and nodded as she continued to push up on the desktop. The slats moved with a groan and a squeal. The other two ghosts, Joe and Great-Uncle Jack, glared at Bree.

"You gonna put some moves into it, girl?" Joe asked. "Or do we have to wait an eternity for you to figure out what's going on in West Landry?"

"Do we have to tell you everything?" Great-Uncle Jack asked. "Kids today. They don't know what to do without the help of those of us caught in limbo."

Bree wrinkled her nose at the two men. "Nana was right. You two went off to war and came back a couple of sourpusses."

The expression was Nana Emily's way of explaining how Joe and

Great-Uncle Jack acted in the week between the time they arrived back in West Landry and when they disappeared. From what Bree had learned today, she now knew her great-uncle never left town, but no one had ever found his body.

"Another mystery." Bree turned back to the desk. "Just what I don't need."

She concentrated on the bigger mystery: who had started all the fires since the summer of '65. Her first task was gaining access to a desk as old as the house, both of which were built in the late 1800s. The rolltop finally latched into place at the top, and she stared at the dozen small drawers on each side of the area of divided shelves and writing space. Bree searched each drawer of the desk but couldn't locate a box where Nana kept important stuff. Stumped, Bree slumped into the rolling chair as old as the desk.

"A box couldn't fit in any of those drawers," Bree said. "They're so small. Even the pens, pencils, and paper clips crowd them."

She rocked the chair forward but then stopped. The wheels creaked and groaned. The sound of wood shifting under the chair turned into a warning when she heard splintering. Bree looked down at the floor.

"What is that?" She stood and shoved the chair away with one foot.

A small throw rug beneath where the chair had been had a very unusual-looking bump, or maybe a lump, in the center. Bree dropped to her knees and lifted the rug. Her eyes widened as she discovered a square cut into the heart of pine floor, a square with a large, blackened metal ring set into the planks.

"A hiding place?" Bree tugged on the ring.

The ring resisted her first efforts but, like the desk, finally gave way; and she opened the door to what appeared to be a treasure trove. There wasn't much in the small hole between the floor and the foundation, but every single piece held her interest. Bree lifted out a large album of photographs and a faded red book with "MY DIARY" etched across the cover in peeling gold letters. Her fingers closed around the first of two boxes, this one metal. It had a lock on the top that stumped her, and Bree set the box aside to deal with at a later time. She then reached for a box that gave off the slight scent of cedar. A gold-tone latch held the lid in place, and Bree began to open it but stopped.

"I have to show all this to Miz Mazie," Bree said.

She gathered the treasure trove into a pile and sought out one of the canvas bags she used for shopping. Once Bree had everything packed, she started for the door but returned to the desk. Another search of the small drawers, this one involving dumping everything onto the writing area, produced a small, thin key that fit the lock on the metal box.

Once she had everything she believed she needed, Bree hurried out the door and not only remembered to shut it, she checked to make sure the lock engaged by rattling the knob. Satisfied that she'd secured her house and made sure no one could get in without doing a lot of damage and making a lot of noise, Bree almost ran across the street. She passed through the ghosts and heard their appreciative comments.

"She's smart, this baby girl," a male ghost said.

"We won't have to wait much longer," a female spirit said with a sigh. "I can see heaven calling us now."

Bree's lips curled upward into a smile as she walked onto Miz Mazie's porch and knocked on her door. One of the neighbors Bree had seen with the elderly woman answered.

"What do you want, baby girl?" the woman asked. "Mazie ain't up to visitors, not after learning her brother's fate like she did."

"She'll want to see me." Bree held up the shopping bag, bulging with her discoveries. "I think I know who and why, but only Miz Mazie can tell me for sure."

The woman turned and spoke with someone behind her.

"Let my baby girl in," Miz Mazie said. "Maybe she's finally found the answers to all our questions."

Bree walked into the house and set her bag on the floor. She gathered Miz Mazie into a long hug and knew this woman would help in the quest to end the mystery of the fires, disappearances, and deaths.

"I think I found something," Bree whispered into Miz Mazie's ear. "But I want you to look at it with me." She broke free of the hug and brought the cedar box out of the canvas bag. "Do you recognize this?"

Holding her breath in anticipation, Bree gave the box to Miz Mazie. Miz Mazie took the box with trembling hands and released the tiny gold latch.

"This be Miz Emily's remembrance box," Miz Mazie said. "Her mama gave her this box the day she married your pa-paw, baby girl."

The elderly woman lifted the lid, and Bree glanced down. Bree's breath caught in her throat. Right on top of the pile of papers and pictures were the same two photographs today's burglar had destroyed.

Bree reached into the box and removed the pictures of her parents, and Jack and Joe. She hadn't lost them after all.

"What are these?" Miz Mazie reached into the box with her free hand and came up with a thick stack of Polaroid pictures. "Why did Emily take pictures of all those fires?"

Shaking with fear, Bree set the two precious photographs on a table beside Miz Mazie's flower print sofa and took the Polaroids. Nana Emily had never wanted a digital camera, even though she would have had the opportunity to save her pictures to a computer.

"I have always loved instant photographs," Nana Emily had said only last Christmas, after Bree had given her a simple digital camera. "I love you, darling Bree, but I won't ever give up my Polaroid camera."

Bree examined each of the pictures, nearly a hundred in all, and figured out the theme immediately. Most were old, spanning a time period from the sixties to three days before she went into assisted living.

"These are evidence." Bree squinted to make out the men in each of the pictures. "And I now have the proof I need to have those men arrested."

Shocked gasps rang through the room. Bree looked up into the startled gazes of six very frightened elderly women. Miz Mazie waved a hand at the group and grinned at Bree.

"I'm a thinking that your nana would be right proud of you, Bree," Miz Mazie said, startling Bree by using her name instead of baby girl. "You do the right thing. We'll stand behind you."

She faced her friends and put her hands on her hips. One by one, the women nodded agreement to the silent demand.

"Okay." Bree put the photographs carefully back into the box and closed the lid. She was worried some of the older pictures might not be good enough. The photos had faded, and some of the ink had reddened, making it hard to discern that it really was Zachariah watching houses burn. "One of you keep a watch for Logan. He's been driving up and down the street."

As if her words were a siren call, the sound of Logan's car engine drifted past the house. Bree took out her cell phone and called Kevin. Kevin couldn't really do anything, but his boss could. Fire Chief Hiram Jameson was also the public safety director, which meant if there was a problem with the police department, he could deal with the issue without having to go to the sheriff.

"Hey, Bree," Kevin said. "I'll be there in a few. The chief let me off early."

Bree started to answer, but an explosion followed by a great whoosh blew out all the windows at the front of Miz Mazie's house. The ladies hurried outside, and Bree followed. She stared at her house, fully engulfed in flames.

"No, you're not," Bree said to Kevin. "My house is on fire."

"Get out!" Kevin shouted. "Drop everything and get out, Bree."

"I am out," she said.

"Hey, Chief," Kevin hollered instead of responding to her. "Put out an alarm for 1313 West Main. Bree's house. It's on fire."

"Okay, Kevin, I'm out," Bree said. "Are you listening to me?"

"We'll be there in three minutes, Bree," Kevin said. "Where are you?"

"Miz Mazie's," Bree said, and started to continue but the phone went dead. "Fire department's on the way," she announced to the older women. "I guess we have to stay here."

The fire trucks arrived in record time, and Bree started to walk off the porch as soon as she saw Kevin speaking with the chief. Both men stared at her house and pointed at the flames spurting from every window and door.

"I didn't really hear Bree," Kevin said as she got near them. "I'm not sure if she's in the house or not, Chief."

"She's out," Bree said, and grinned when Kevin spun around. "She wasn't in there when it blew up." She frowned. "And I don't understand why—"

Her breath caught in her throat when she smelled the unmistakable odor of gasoline, an extremely heavy odor of gasoline. But her most important task was to stop the Sandowski men before they burned another home. Even though she no longer had a place to live, Bree was more interested in stopping the fires in West Landry.

"I know who the arsonist is," Bree announced. "And I have evidence in Miz Mazie's house to prove Zachariah, Benjamin, and Logan Sandowski set all these fires." She took and released a deep breath. "Going all the way back to the summer of '65, when my great-uncle died." Bree faced the fire chief. "I know you have arrest powers. Do your duty. Look at the evidence and then arrest those men."

Chief Jameson took Bree back into Miz Mazie's house. He looked over the pictures and shook his head.

"Can't argue with these pictures," Chief Jameson said. "But the Sandowskis supposedly left town after we put out the theater fire. Let me see if we can get the state police to find them."

He went back outside. Bree, Miz Mazie, and all the other women followed him in time to see Logan, Benjamin, and Zachariah cruise past the burning house.

"Stop them!" Bree screamed, and reached for a rock.

To her amazement, the people of West Landry darted out of their homes and blocked the Sandowskis. Chief Jameson pulled all three men from their vehicle and arrested them.

"Wasn't us!" Logan howled. "It was Bree. We saw her blowing up her house."

"With what?" Miz Mazie demanded. "Tell us what my baby girl used to blow up the house she loves?"

"Dynamite," Logan answered.

Benjamin and Zachariah nodded and began making the same outrageous claim. Bree laughed.

"I wasn't even in the house when it blew up," Bree said. "And the evidence of your crimes is in Chief Jameson's hands."

The chief held up the photographs, and it was as if a great cloud lifted from West Landry. Every single man, woman, and child came forth to shout out what they'd seen but had been too afraid to admit. Bree turned away from the noise and watched as the firefighters worked to stop the fire destroying her house from attacking the buildings on either side of it. A feeling of great loss ran through her. The only house she'd ever lived in was no longer hers. She had no place to live.

"Hey, Bree." Kevin joined her. "I know it's kind of weird, but you can stay at my place until you find a new home."

It was weird, but also very sweet of him. Kevin lived in a cramped, one-bedroom apartment near the fire station.

"Oh no!" Miz Mazie inserted herself between them. "My baby girl ain't gonna live nowhere but with me. She ain't gonna take up with no boy until you say your vows."

Bree's face flushed red. She gave up arguing about where to stay, just as she'd given up long ago on trying to make everyone in West Landry stop calling her baby girl. Some things were never meant to change.

KC SPRAYBERRY is a writer of westerns, romance, young adult, and middle grade stories. She lives in northwest Georgia with her husband and youngest child. Her work has appeared in various print and online magazines, and she was one of the *Mystery Times Ten 2011* authors. Her new book, *Softly Say Goodbye*, will be released soon by Solstice Publishing.

You can contact her on Facebook under her name, twitter @ kcsowriter, her website: www.KCSprayberry.com, or read her blog at: outofcontrolcharactes.blogspot.com.

The Disappearance of Belle Robbins

Johanna Harness

MY FIRST REAL memory was fear.

Frank Tully twisted the big dial on the radio, and folks at the community potluck froze, forks halfway to their mouths. In utter silence, everyone leaned in to hear the announcer's words.

At five years old, I didn't understand. "What happened?" I asked. When no one answered, I asked again. Other than the crackle on the airwaves, my tiny voice was the only sound.

An older woman, one of those who said "Children should be seen, not heard," turned toward me. Her skin bunched up in deep wrinkles when she smiled. Her eyes danced. "They killed the Lindbergh baby," she said. Then she winked. "You best be a good girl and hush or they'll kill you too."

I didn't know who that baby was or who killed him, but I hightailed it out of the Dry Lake Community Center as fast as my legs would carry me. When my mother found me hiding in a tractor shed, I collapsed into her arms, shaking and crying and begging her not to let them get me.

All during my childhood, adults trotted out the story of how Myrtle Tully scared the bejesus out of Annie MacPherson, how that stupid kid thought baby murderers would traipse all the way to Washington State to demand ransom from a struggling sheep rancher.

I tried not to react, but the same thing always happened. The story kept growing—longer and more agonizing—until they made the tears well up and made me look away. Then someone always poked me in the ribs, laughed gleefully, and told me to toughen up. Eventually I did.

Twelve years later, I threw off my warm covers and ignored the way the frigid air made my lungs hurt and my shoulders spasm. I rubbed a sleeve back and forth across my nose and eyes and then patted my upper body. Buckles. Straps. I'd slept in my overalls then. Good for me.

Of course, Mother would complain like she always did. "Annie!" she'd scold. "You're ruining my good, white sheets!"

Whatever. Mother wasn't the one getting up around the clock to feed bawling lambs.

I dropped my feet into waiting boots and made my way down to the porch. When I'd first reported Belle Robbins missing, not even her parents believed me. They said I had abduction issues, and Belle didn't like being tied down. She'd turn up. No need to worry.

After my friend had been gone a week, Dry Lake quivered with gossip. Now, after two weeks, it seemed there were some folks who'd like nothing better than the entertainment of a local girl turning up dead.

I shivered and looked out toward the shadow of the barn. I couldn't be the only teenage girl to feel it: that sense that the community might sacrifice any of us for a little news of blood.

I rubbed my arms, stomped my feet, and tried to get my teeth to quit chattering. Nothing seemed amiss. It was a dark morning just like any other. I couldn't see any reason to think danger lurked nearby. Of course, that might have been what Belle thought right before she vanished.

Disgusted by my skittishness, I plunged off the porch, covering the distance to the barn in long strides. The flicker of dim bulbs meant food to the bummers. They bounced up and cried, frantically nosing the air in case they'd missed the nearness of a bottle. Just as I paused to speak to them, I glanced to the back of the barn and saw the rise of steam.

Heading straight toward it, nudging my way through a sea of cream-colored sheep, I had to smile. The combined smells of new straw and wet wool and fresh milk comforted me like nothing else. This was my place, and I belonged here. Plus? All those ewes were on my side. If anyone lurked in the darkness, ready to grab me and haul me away, I'd know by the way they reacted.

The old women in our community would have been quick to point out the selfish nature of my thoughts. The sheep provided an answer for me, but what about everyone else? We were all more vulnerable with "our men" gone off to war. That's the way they always talked. Our values. Our girls. Our flag. My Michael. My Jules. My William.

Just the other day, Myrtle Tully held down her spot at the big quilting frame, pronouncing judgment: "If my Frank were here, he'd take care of our Belle Robbins problem in a hurry."

My little sister, Mary, ran back and forth under the frame, tapping knees and darting from one point to another. She pretended to play but was really absorbing every detail. I'd enlisted her as my spy, and she reported everything to me in hushed whispers.

"What could Frank do?" Elsa asked. "You think he'd watch over all the girls, do ya? He's good that way? Knows what they're all doing?"

Mary imitated Myrtle's expression, and I laughed. I doubted the old woman really looked so much like a horse. "What did she say?" I asked my sister.

Mary stuck her nose up in the air and put hands on her hips. She made her voice stiff and squeaky. 'My Frank would stop this nonsense. That girl isn't missing. She run off. End of story.'

"Sheriff says different," I said.

Mary nodded enthusiastically. "That's what Elsa said! But then Myrtle, she said that Sheriff Daggett is a fool and couldn't tell a squirrel from a rabbit."

That last part might have been true. The sheriff wore bottle glasses and stumbled a lot. He'd volunteered to fight for our country, but apparently the men at the enlistment office thought it better he keep pointing his gun at locals rather than other men with guns. I didn't see any reason to think Daggett was a fool though. Or maybe I just thought being a fool was a relative kind of thing.

Those local boys who ran around talking nonsense fit my definition. "I'm gonna kill me some Japs," Jonny Nelsen would say. Then he and his friends would go shoot up the woods and come home carrying pitiful animals that hadn't deserved to die.

If Myrtle needed some fools, she might look to them. Instead, the old woman just smiled. "Boys will be boys." That's what she said. For everything else? "Things would be different if my Frank were here."

When I saw the struggling ewe, I discarded my thoughts of Myrtle. The yearling lay flat on her side, nose raised high in the air, pushing. There on the ground behind her was a huge, black lamb. Steam rose from his unmoving body.

"S'okay. S'okay," I said, not really sure it was.

I prepared to find the newborn stiff and cooling rapidly. Instead, the boy lurched under my fingertips. I swear I jumped back a foot or more, gulping air and blinking like crazy. Jeez. What was wrong with me? I had to get my nerves in check.

Hands shaking, I rubbed the lamb all over. When he bleated, I moved him up by his mama's head and checked her other end.

"Let's see how you're doing."

Ugh. One gangly leg hung all the way out, straw sticking to a tiny black hoof. Above it was a nose and two hooves. The ewe pushed, but no way could that second lamb make it around the first.

"I'm sorry," I whispered.

Then I did what had to be done. Supporting the fragile bones of the dangling leg with one hand, I pushed on the born-too-soon hoof, forcing it back up inside the mama's body. Elbow deep, I pushed that lamb behind the other and watched the ewe's huge belly bulge and flip.

As I pulled my arm back out, I wrapped thumb and pinkie around two hooves and brought them along. Amniotic fluid soaked my legs and feet as the lamb broke free. I dropped her in the straw by the ewe's head, turned back, and there was the gangly leg again, and a tail. This wasn't ideal.

As quickly as I could, I eased a hand inside, found the other leg, and pulled. The big thing came out to the middle, but the shoulders wouldn't budge. Twisting side to side did no good, so I stood, braced myself, and tugged so hard I feared that lamb would break in two.

When the big-shouldered boy finally gave way, I stumbled backward, still holding him by slippery back legs. I dropped him in the straw, pulled the membranes from his face, checked his mouth, and rubbed him all over. He didn't move.

"Come on."

Grabbing the big lamb by the back legs, I judged the distance to roof and floor and threw him diagonally overhead, into a spin. At the bottom of the swing, I let the centrifugal force pull him back up and around again. At the bottom of that circle, his body jerked, and I almost dropped him.

Under his mother's nose, he came to life. As she nudged and talked in wet bleats, the boy's legs began kicking. He lifted his head, and I swear he smiled when his mother licked the side of his face.

I sat back on my heels, leaning against the barn wall. The first lamb had already wandered away on weak legs, stumbling, falling, and springing up again. The second lamb struggled to stand. All three were bigger than they should have been. All three were blacker than they should have been.

I'd grown up ranching, and I knew these things. While other girls wandered after their mothers, dragging dolls in the dirt, learning women's work, Belle and I did all we could to keep our place among the men.

We'd watched older girls, so we knew how it would go. As soon as our figures drew attention, our days were numbered. If even one older man blushed while we hunkered over a ewe, we'd be back at our mothers' sides quicker than they could whistle for us. Our time among the sheep would be over.

So Belle and I? We decided not to attract attention. We bought too-big overalls to hide our hips, and we helped each other bind long strips of muslin around our chests, pinning the sides with diaper pins. We kept our hair tucked under caps and adopted as many boyish mannerisms as we could: strutting while we talked, swiping dirty hands across our legs, wiping our noses on our sleeves. We kept our faces smudged, giggled only with each other, and always avoided talking to the boys our age.

As for me, I had to take special care around Caleb Nelsen. For more than a year now, the boy had been making my knees go weak, making me smile from cheek to cheek and forget myself. Belle saved me more than once, steering me away from him. Now Caleb strutted around talking about enlisting, and all the older girls swooned around him. Stupid Caleb. At least I wouldn't have to worry about his curly blond hair or his dimples much longer.

Plus, Caleb leaving before the summer meant that my daddy was short a man to drive sheep. Last year Daddy had complained about sending out boys to do a man's work; but, according to Mary, this year he contemplated sending out a girl: me!

"She's better than any of the boys." That's what Mary said he'd told our mother.

"No, Albert, not Annie. Not after what happened with Belle. I'll never stop worrying."

"What else can we do?" he'd asked. "Honestly? If Belle was here, I'd send her too. Now that she's gone, I'm still short."

"Albert! How can you be worried about sheep when a girl is missing?" Mary frowned.

"What?" I asked. "What did he say?"

"Nothing."

Oh. Mary and I both knew what that meant. In our house, arguments amounted to deafening silence and crossed arms.

"Take me with you," Mary pleaded.

I looked at my little sister's perfect ringlets and the ruffled apron tied around her flour sack dress. "You're her little doll," I said. "She already has your future planned."

Mary shook her shoulders as if she wanted to wriggle out of her skin. "Someday I'm going to run away," she whispered. "And I ain't looking back. Not for anything."

I pursed my lips. "Someday you'll get married and settle down and running will mean leaving behind your six kids and your favorite donkey and you'll stay put, whispering to your daughters about how they should follow their dreams."

Oh, that look she gave me! And oh, the silence that followed.

Mary folded her arms, stared long and hard into my eyes, and then walked away. It had been fifty-two hours since she stared me down. No telling how long before she'd speak again.

Fine. Maybe I'd be gone before she got over it, and then she could sit and stew without me.

The big lamb kicked and struggled. I rocked forward and lifted him to his feet, but he fell again.

Three black lambs from this ewe alone. I still couldn't believe it. In an average year, only one out of two hundred lambs would be black. I knew this well, because that's how we counted sheep on a drive. If a single black ewe disappeared, that meant another hundred ninety-nine disappeared with her—and we'd have to go find them.

Daddy always said the black lambs were good luck, and with times being so tough, he called all these miracles. Still, the man was no fool. I'm sure he had suspicions.

I know I did. And it wasn't just the percentages bothering me. I'd taught Mary all she knew about spying, and I used my skills to hang on Caleb Nelsen's every word—from behind the corner of a shed, so as not to attract unwanted attention. That's where I was when I heard Caleb and Smitty sniggering about the lamb crop.

"Quite the night's work," Smitty said.

Caleb fake-coughed. "Thirty-two so far. Think we should tell the old man?"

"And take away his miracle?" Smitty laughed. "We did the guy a favor."

"He's lost stock."

"Not our fault," said Smitty. "Shepherdesses belong in nursery rhymes, not on the range. Belle Robbins couldn't cut it."

Caleb didn't answer right away. "The lambs are too big," he finally said. "That's not Belle's fault."

Smitty snorted. "You want a turn with her? Hell, I don't blame you. I've had my fun. I'll loan her to you. Don't act like she can do a man's work though. I know for a fact she's soft—in all the right places."

I peeked around the building in time to see Smitty outlining the shape of a woman's body with his hands and then making a rude gesture with his hips. When Caleb punched him, the boy seemed a lot more surprised than I was. When Smitty pulled himself off the ground, fists jabbing at Caleb's ducking head, I made tracks in the opposite direction.

I didn't tell Belle about Smitty's bragging. Boys will be boys, right? He lied. And Caleb decked him, which pretty much evened up the score. I did, however, tell Belle the rest of what I'd heard.

It all made sense. Last season, Caleb and Smitty took bands of sheep across eastern Washington, into Idaho, where they shipped market lambs by rail. They combined their smaller flocks for the trip back, lingering in the wheat fields of the Palouse, allowing the sheep to clear the stubble.

Somewhere on their way home, those boys introduced another ram to our ewes. It was the only thing that made any sense. Our regular rams did not throw lambs like these.

If Belle and I had been regular tenders, I doubt this would have happened. As it was, we only managed part-time status. We took the wagons out and kept the drivers stocked with food, but my mother insisted we not stay and cook for the men. Daddy could ignore our fragile female qualities only as long as his wife approved—and she deemed the isolated camps inappropriate. If I'd been there, those boys would have been more responsible with my father's sheep.

Exhaling, I leaned forward and wiped bloody hands across my overalls. It was time for me to remember my own responsibilities. I had to find that wandering lamb, get the ewe and newborns into a jug, and feed those bummers.

Grasping the two remaining lambs by hind legs, I pulled them gently through the straw. The ewe grunted and pushed herself to her feet, taking steps to catch up. When she called out, the lambs called back and squirmed. I kept pulling them along the barn floor.

I backed them all the way into a jug, let myself out, and waited for the ewe. She cried for her lambs but kept staring at the corner where she'd given birth. I nudged her inside and latched the gate.

"I'll get him," I promised.

The bum lambs heard my voice and jumped to their feet again, calling loudly for their bottles.

"In a minute."

I made my way through the darkness, against the movement of the expectant flock. Ewes grunted, pushed heavy bodies onto fragile hooves, and swayed toward me. That silly lamb must be making a nuisance of himself if none of the sheep wanted to be back there with him.

I smiled at first—and then I worried. My confidence rooted itself in the knowledge that these sheep would react to a disturbance, warning me of any danger. This was a reaction.

I blinked and scolded myself. Darkness and lack of sleep played games with my mind.

And there! Just listen. The newborn called out to me with desperate bleats. He'd clearly gotten stuck. That's why he hadn't returned to his mother earlier. I really had nothing to worry about.

And anyway, how many times had my father told me: "Fear is no excuse for not doing those things that got to be done."

The first time he told me that, I wasn't much more than eight years old. A storm had come up out of nowhere, picking up speed as it went, and our old windmill rattled and rolled like crazy. Spinning like that, no way was it producing electricity. Something had pulled lose. It took two people to slip it out of gear and tie it down, and I was the only one available to help.

"No, Daddy." Tears poured down my face, and dirt blew into those tears. "I'm afraid of heights." He put the rope around my middle and forced my hands onto the rope.

"You're all I've got." He sounded sorry, but more sorry I wasn't a boy than he was sorry for what he was about to make me do. "Fear is no excuse for not doing those things that got to be done."

I shook the whole way up, the whole time we settled the mill against increasing winds, and the whole way back down; but I did what I was told.

Later Daddy wouldn't even look me in the eye. "Don't tell your mother," he said.

I never did. I never told anyone—not even Belle. Since then, however, I've compared every stupid fear to climbing a windmill in gale-force winds. Why should I be jumpy about going after a stuck lamb when I'd been through so much worse?

Maybe I'd have exercised more caution if it wasn't for the windmill experience. Maybe I'd have turned around and left right then, and I'd have never known what happened to Belle Robbins.

Instead, I made myself stand up tall, and I marched toward that back corner, disturbing more sheep as I went. By then the barn walls shook with the sound of bleating babies, all calling for their mothers. It's not surprising I couldn't hear much else.

The errant newborn had to be somewhere in that corner. When I couldn't find him, I checked around doors and finally knelt down to look in the space between troughs. And there was the lamb—nosing a crouching, shadowed figure.

Shrieking, I lurched backward as the man jumped toward me. I remember thinking it was the strangest thing that someone wanting to kill me would be cradling that lamb so gently in his arms. And I remember registering that fact long before I realized the man was Japanese.

Once he was clear of the feeder, we reacted identically. Our eyes wide with fear, we took steps back from each other. He sized up my appearance as I sized up his. We were about the same height and about the same age, about the same amount of scared.

"Don't hurt me," we both said.

I looked from side to side, wondering if there was someone else present. What power could he think I had? I grabbed a bucket and held it out in front of my body, like a warning. I'm not exactly sure what the warning was, but I adopted a stance that said "I have a bucket, and I'm not afraid to use it."

The newborn lamb bleated and squirmed, and I startled, stabbing the air with the bucket. "What do you want?"

"Belle," he whispered.

Breath caught in my throat. "What have you done with her?"

He gently lowered the lamb to the barn floor. His words, soft and deep, comforted me. "No. No. It's not like that." He glanced toward the door. "We were supposed to meet—Belle and I. She didn't show up." He extended a hand. "I'm Henry. You're Annie?"

I narrowed my eyes. "How could you know that?"

"How could I not? She described you perfectly. You're why I'm here." He pushed his hand toward me again.

Only when I saw my hand in his did the differences between us really hit home. This much contact between us would wreak havoc with my neighbors. I let go quickly.

"What do you want from me?"

Henry nodded toward the door. "Maybe we should get those lambs some milk before someone comes to check on you."

I stood there, completely still, unable to think what to do. Henry waited patiently for me to make up my mind, but the lamb did not. The newborn wobbled over and repeatedly jabbed his nose into my leg until I picked him up. I took him to his jug, and Henry followed.

"Belle helped me," Henry said. "That was all we ever meant it to be."

I dared a glance in his direction before letting myself into a pen where a ewe stamped the ground. I leaned against her and eased the fullness from her udder before taking all the milk I could get. Her single lamb would still have plenty.

Back outside the jug, I poured milk into a bottle and handed it to Henry. "How did she help you?"

"I was lost." He lifted a bawling lamb and rubbed her head until she latched. "Belle helped me find my way." Another quick look at me and he repeated, "That was all we ever meant it to be."

"Last summer?" I asked.

"Yes, but I'd been headed there for months. Soldiers searched our house and took my father. I kept thinking it was all a big mistake. These things didn't happen in America. I thought they'd send him home, but they never did. He wrote us letters from a place called Kooskia. He said they kept him with other prisoners, building roads. I thought I could go there and explain. My father did not belong with prisoners. Those books and swords in our house were family heirlooms. Never was there a more gentle man. My father would never do anything to harm this country. If they knew him, if they knew my family, they'd let him go."

I placed a long board over the top of several bottles, securing the lids and nipples through small openings. When I flipped the feeder down into the pen, the remaining lambs found their spots.

"You're saying Belle knew how to get to Kooskia?"

Henry smiled. "No. She helped me find my way by convincing me to go home."

"Which is where?"

"Near Spokane."

"So that's it? She talked sense into you, and you hightailed it home?"

"No." He lowered his eyes. "We spent the rest of the summer together."

I slammed the milk bucket down on the counter and set my jaw.

"Are you kidding me?" My words came out somewhere between a whisper and a hiss. "What were you thinking? You both had to know that couldn't work out!"

"We were thinking we wanted to be married."

"In Idaho? It's not even legal."

"That's why we planned to meet in Washington."

"You're saying she ran off to elope? With you?"

"I'm saying she was supposed to run off, to elope with me; but she never showed up. I came here to find her and saw all those signs about the missing girl."

I stared at him, trying to calculate how much of a fool I was to be standing there, believing his words, not screaming for help. "Maybe she decided not to elope. Maybe you came here and kidnapped her."

Henry blinked at me. "If that was the case, why would I be here asking for your help?"

"I found you hiding. How do I know you ever intended to talk to me?"

Henry handed over the lamb he'd been cuddling. "You're very distrustful," he said. Then he walked out the doorway.

I dropped the lamb down into the pen. "Wait, Henry. I'm sorry." I rushed to catch up, shutting off the barn light as I left. "Where do you think she's gone?"

He stopped and waited for me. We stood in the darkness longer than I felt comfortable.

"This isn't easy for me," he said.

"What isn't easy?"

"I do think it's possible Belle had second thoughts, but not in the way you think."

I curled my arms around each other. "I'm getting cold, Henry. Get to the point."

He sighed then—and it wasn't one of those normal, okay-fine sighs. It was one of those deep-release-grief sighs—the kind heard at funerals just before they closed the lid forever.

"Is there somewhere you would go..." He took a few deep breaths. "Is there a doctor?"

"Doc Krill is in town. He treats everyone. Are you hurt?"

"No, please. Hear what I'm asking. If you changed your mind about becoming a mother, is there a doctor?"

My mind slipped into a spin. "You're saying she was expecting?"

"She thought she might be. We planned to meet before anything became obvious."

I blinked into the darkness. Maybe those baggy overalls benefitted Belle more than I realized. Still? No. Not Belle. First Smitty bragged like that and now this.

Or was it the other way around? First this?

Belle had to know she had no real future with Henry. What if Smitty was her backup plan?

"Annie?"

"Hmm? What?"

"I asked if you knew of a doctor."

"Me? How would I know something like that?"

"Girls talk. You're Belle's friend."

"I wouldn't know. She didn't say anything to me about you or her condition—or anything. Girls apparently don't talk as much as you think they do."

"Please," Henry whispered. "What if she's missing because she needs medical attention?"

I closed my eyes and rubbed fingers into my temples. There was something—some talk about a school teacher a few years ago. The older girls said the midwife had gone to see her; and I was young and stupid, and I said, "I didn't even know she was going to have a baby" and the oldest girl said, "She's not." Then another girl said, "Not anymore," and they all shushed her.

"The midwife," I told Henry. "She might be the one."

"Take me to her."

"Oh no," My eyes flew open. "No. I'm not going anywhere with you. You go back home, and I'll let you know."

"You think I came this far to go home?"

From up by the house came the sound of my daddy's raspy cough and the heavy stomp of boots. The screen door slammed, and I watched a tiny flare and then the steady glow from a cigarette.

I pulled Henry back into the shadows and pointed behind us. "You stay in the sheep wagon. I'll be as quick as I can; but shearers come today, and Daddy'll need me in the lambing shed. You may have to wait a bit."

"I'm sure Belle's sorry to inconvenience you with her misfortune."

I sucked in air, ready to give him what-for, but the flickering of the barn light distracted me.

"Annie, you out here?"

"Go," I whispered to Henry, but he was already gone. I heard a faint click of the sheep wagon door and rushed over to meet Daddy.

"Annie!" he called again.

"No need to yell. I'm right here."

He cleared his throat and scrubbed his boot in the dirt.

"Yearling had big triplets this morning," I said.

Daddy stared at me. "How many'd we lose?"

"So far, so good."

He glanced at the blood on my arms and my overalls. I thought he looked faintly pleased with me, but it was hard to tell.

"I know there's still work to do," I said. "I was just catching some fresh air while I had the chance."

"You'll catch your death soaked head to toe out in that wind." He took a long drag on his cigarette. "If that doesn't kill you, your mother will." He paused and looked me over again. I nodded. We understood each other.

Squinting up into the dark sky behind me, he pulled smoke into his lungs. After a slow exhale he said, "You know I want to send you out this summer."

A ridiculous grin surfaced, and I pushed it back. This was my big break. I couldn't mess it up, acting like a girl. "Yes, sir," I said.

His eyes darted toward me before he returned his gaze to the sky. "After what happened to Belle, I'm not sure I can do it."

I wanted to wail. I wanted to cry and stomp and tell him he couldn't do this to me, but I knew better. Weakness never solved anything.

"You've got work needs done," I said. "I can do that work."

The corner of his mouth twitched. "Reckon that's true."

"Shearing crew coming today?" I asked.

"Yep."

"I could use the stretch. You want me to ride down to Melnick's—see if they can lend us their kids?"

I didn't have to tell him how much the little ones could help during the culling and the splitting. He already knew that. I didn't have to tell him the Melnicks lived just past the midwife. He didn't need to know everything.

"That'd be fine," he said.

I didn't give Daddy a chance to reconsider. By the time the sun came up, I was halfway to my destination, still trying to figure out Belle's math. If she'd met Henry on his way from Spokane to Kooskia, the earliest they got together was midsummer. Maybe the first of July. Of course, if the boy was really, truly lost, who knew where or when they'd met. I could have asked, but the idea of it made me blush.

When the midwife's house came into view, I still hadn't put the pieces together. By September, the ewes were cleaning up Palouse stubble. By mid September, when the rams arrived, Henry should have been heading north. If Belle had suspicions—oh no. That meant she was due anytime now!

Wait, no, that wasn't right, because Belle wasn't a sheep.

Sheep had the sense to produce young in five months. And their young could walk and talk and wander off twenty minutes after birth. Humans took more time. If Belle missed one of her monthlies by the time the rams arrived—and sheep were lambing now—that put my friend at six months along. Seven if she'd missed two courses.

I wasn't quite sure how long it took to grow a human, but, if this was true, Belle had to be hiding a significant belly under those overalls. I didn't think she'd go to the midwife—not this far along—not for the reasons Henry suspected.

I dismounted, hitched the reins to a post, and made my way to the midwife's porch. Before I reached the door, it squeaked open. I hopped up the stairs, expecting to be greeted by a heavyset woman with a baby on her shoulder. Instead? Myrtle Tully stood there, shotgun aimed at my chest.

"Guess you'd better come in," she said. "Keep your hands where I can see 'em."

For the second time that day, I wasn't sure how anyone imagined I could be a danger. This time I didn't even have a bucket.

"Let her go!" Mattie Halstead, the midwife, sat in a chair by the fire. Her hair looked ratty, and her face was covered with soot.

Myrtle turned the shotgun on her. "Didn't ask you for advice, did I?"

My heart raced. Surely I had some things going for me. Like my horse was still tied up outside.

Myrtle jerked the shotgun at Mattie. "Go untie the horse," she said.

Dang.

Myrtle aimed at me again. "Be quick or this one dies."

I watched Mattie run out and untie the reins, flicking them up and over the saddle. It didn't really matter to the old mare. She'd been doing what she pleased for years. When Mattie swatted at her, the horse took a few steps forward and stopped to munch weeds.

I covered my mouth to hide my smile, but Myrtle saw it. Quicker than I knew she could move, the old woman darted out onto that porch, shot into the sky—and my horse took off.

Myrtle motioned Mattie back in the house before unleashing anger on me. "You and your friend think you're smarter than me, but you're wrong. If my Frank was here, things would be different. You girls wouldn't think you could get by with your nonsense."

I blinked at her. My friend? So Belle really was here? Up until that moment I wasn't convinced. I'd been treating this as yet another Crazy Myrtle episode. "You?" I asked. "You kidnapped Belle? She's here?"

"Of course she's here," said Myrtle. "And she's staying here. She was fixin' to run off with my grandson's baby."

Myrtle had like fourteen kids. And each of those kids had fourteen kids. And half of those had started bearing fruit. Myrtle had a genealogical tie to everyone in town, if not by blood then marriage.

I was pretty sure I could link up to her two or three ways myself. I honestly had no idea who she meant, and when she said, "Marvin Smithers," I still had no idea.

"Smitty," Mattie whispered.

"Abandonment," said Myrtle. "Belle Robbins should know better than to mess with my family. If my Frank was here, he'd set things straight. Since he's not, it's up to me."

I didn't want to take my eyes off the crazy woman, but I glanced at Mattie anyway. "Is Belle okay?"

"Yes. She came to me for swelling in her legs."

Myrtle snapped. "She came to you on her way out of town. I heard it all before you shushed her and told her you weren't alone."

"She should have come to me earlier. Girl was still trying to help with lambing, and she could barely walk." The midwife glared at me. "You didn't notice?"

"No." Jeez. No wonder Belle had trouble pulling lambs. I might have paid attention if I'd suspected her condition. As it was, I didn't think anything of hemming bigger overalls. It's just what we did.

"Smitty's the father?" I started doing Belle's math again, but none of the answers made sense.

Myrtle pursed her lips. "Marvin confided in me. Indiscretions are common with boys heading off to war. He asked if his wife and child could live with me when he enlisted."

"And that's when she run," said Mattie.

"Can I see her?"

"See her?" asked Myrtle. "You're not getting the picture." She jabbed me with the shotgun, pushing me toward a back bedroom. "You just became her nurse."

I wanted to protest as the door closed, but then I saw Belle's eyes: earnest, worried, pleading. I knelt beside her bed and took her hand.

"I really messed things up," she said.

Leaning forward, I whispered in her ear, "Henry's at the ranch."

She gripped my hand so hard it hurt. Her eyes darted toward the door, and she responded in a rush. "No. You lie. I wrote to him. I told him there was no baby, that we should go our own ways. You don't understand how bad this is, Annie. They took his father in the night—because he owned some books and a sword. If they imprison Japanese for that, what will they do to Henry for this?" She pointed to her belly.

"The marriage wouldn't be illegal in Washington," I told her. I couldn't believe I was repeating Henry's words.

"You don't understand the reality of this." She whispered the words in staccato beats.

"So you jumped in bed with Smitty?"

"I jumped the first opportunity I got," said Belle. "It was only when the lambs started coming—it was only then I realized the baby might not look like me. And then Smitty started talking about me living with Myrtle, and I kept thinking about Frank coming home to a Japanese kid living in his house."

I stifled a laugh, and Belle glared at me.

"Sorry. Just picturing Frank's expression." I placed a hand on Belle's tummy, hoping the baby would kick. "Kid's gonna be a looker," I told her. "You're not bad, but that Henry is gorgeous. If you don't want him, I might see if he'll have me. Have you heard his voice?"

Belle closed her eyes and sighed. "Every night in my dreams." She tried not to smile but gave up. "We wanted to get married then. Did he tell you?"

"He still wants to marry you. That's why he's here."

"It's dangerous," said Belle.

A loud thump came from the outer room. "Your future grandmother-in-law kidnapped you and your best friend, and she's holding a gun on the midwife. I'm not sure you have enough distance from all this to properly calculate danger."

"You think I should go with him?"

"I think you already went with him, and now you should see it through."

Belle frowned. "You could say as much about Smitty."

"No," I told her. "One man loves you. The other man wants you to live with his homicidal grandmother. I'm not seeing the parallel."

A noise far away drew me to the window. In the distance were sheep—a lot of sheep, ready for shearing. At the tree line was a sheep wagon—my sheep wagon. Tied to it was a horse—my horse—the very same mare I'd been riding not an hour ago. I leaned so close to the window my nose touched the glass—and that's when Mary's head popped up right in front of my face. I fell backward, thankful I hadn't screamed.

She motioned up with both thumbs, and I lifted the glass. "You're lucky I'm a good spy," she whispered. "Sheriff's on his way. Can Belle walk?"

When Henry popped up behind Mary, we discovered that Belle could walk. Not only that, she could slide right out that window and into her truelove's arms.

That was the last I ever saw of Belle.

When the sheriff came, I pointed to a bed full of pillows and told him the old woman was delusional. He took me aside and told me it was to be expected. It wasn't widely known, but Myrtle's husband Frank died on his way to enlist. He got so worked up about those Japs in Spokane, he fell right down from a heart attack. Myrtle had been coming apart at the seams ever since.

As to what happened to Belle Robbins, the community claimed her disappearance as their one unsolved mystery. Whatever happened to that girl, most say the old woman took the secret to her grave—which, it turns out, was closer than any of us expected.

You see, when Myrtle Tully overheard Sheriff Daggett talking about her late husband, she reacted. Spry—that's how I'd describe that old woman. She could move just like a spring lamb—no setup, just a sudden burst of energy and bounce. She leaped forward, hunkered down, and shot two of the sheriff's toes plum out of his boot.

Poor Daggett. He squinted through his bottle glasses, lifted his gun, and aimed at his assailant's shooting arm. The bullet went straight through what remained of Myrtle's tiny heart.

JOHANNA HARNESS writes and keeps sheep in Idaho. She can pull difficult lambs, detect a ewe in labor from twelve miles away, and replace prolapsed bits that really are as gross as they sound. Despite her comfort in the big red barn, she makes a poor rancher because she gets too attached to the animals. After keeping a sheep in the house for six months, Johanna accepted that she's likely to have more financial success writing than she is with lambs. She's currently working diligently on this nonsheep alternative. You can follow her progress online at johannaharness.com.

The Stash

Sam Hilliard

EYES SAY A lot about a person. Mine say I kill for a living. A modern day Darwin, really. The deals I cut clear out the deadwood and make room for the next wave of evolution.

Biglar's eyes, on the other hand, say she is friendly, loves children, and roots for the underdog. A real do-gooder. It's oversimplifying our relationship to state that I love hating her. Really, I have no choice but to work with Biglar. We're a team. And we are very good at what we do. Maybe to outsiders we seem galaxies apart. In truth, we both excel at our chosen profession.

Some call us vampires because we drain the life out of established communities for personal gain. I resent that charge. First off, the technical term is real estate lawyer. But whatever you like. To critics, we rape the countryside in the name of condominiums and shopping malls. Dirty work for those with a conscience. Fortunately I lack one.

It's Tuesday morning. We're on the way from the airport to a hotel, half asleep, thirty minutes off a redeye from Houston. Here for two days, then off to Cleveland.

All I'm really thinking about now is the man walking toward us on the side of the road, thumbing a ride with his right hand. I imagine what his eyes might say about him. I'm also curious about those who dare to hitchhike in this day and age.

If Jack Kerouac tried hitching rides from New York to Florida today, his publishers would change the title from *On the Road* to *Stuck in Hackensack*. He'd be lucky to make it to the Garden State Parkway. The failure would not be Jack's. Most drivers go out of their way to avoid hitchers, day or night. In fact, there are entire towns in America where hitchhikers walk through a town instead of burning time on the asphalt, because the odds of catching a break are so poor. Until the next freeway exit, Hello, shoe leather express. And these are big towns too—lots bigger than Creskin.

But if it's 2:00 a.m., drizzling, the hitcher is a large, hairy male with a goat head tattooed on his neck, and the town is Creskin, New York, the hitcher's odds of getting out by car approach zero.

Unless the driver comes from someplace where people stop for strangers.

Biglar, the driver, is from far away. She's from Utah. Her parents are missionaries in Zambia. She's naive enough, kind enough, to stop.

Riding shotgun: Hap. Hap Collins. That's me. For the record, I am not the sort to stop for strangers, much less help them. I want to be clear about that point.

Biglar slows the car, and we have a clear view of the hitcher ten feet away. He looks more menacing up close.

I let Biglar know it's a bad idea to stop for him. And not just because he's a stranger. And not just because a security alarm inside a nearby sporting good shop clatters in the night.

No, it's the fresh bloodstains on his duffel bag that unnerve me.

2

BIGLAR FORGIVES THE bloodied bag and turns on the hazard lights. Damage to the interior is a nonissue. The car is a rental, and she paid the twenty-two dollar, no-liability surcharge. Even if she returns the car in pieces, she is covered.

"We should be running over this guy," I say. "Not picking him up."

"He needs our help," Biglar says. Expect nothing less from a missionary's daughter, I guess. She goes for the kill when it matters, but above all she's more sweet than vicious. I guess that's a good thing, but in moments like this, a defect of character like that is a real pain. Biglar eases off the gas.

I grip the metal lever of the door handle. "Pull in close on the right. I can swipe him with the door."

Having none of my logic, she steers the car too far away from the shoulder. "Can you fake being human for a minute?" she asks.

"Did humanity close the Tyrell deal yesterday?" A personal favorite of mine, the development will replace a hundred small, old homes with a hotel and strip mall. I support the deal for the rightest of reasons. I want a second vacation home in Maui.

"We need to talk about that later, Hap. There may be other considerations we overlooked during the planning phase." She pauses. "I'm not sure those people will move on quietly."

"I've heard that property rights rap before," I say. "And when push comes to shove, when the bulldozers land on their street, they take the buyout before the roof comes off." The hitcher walks toward us. The weight of the duffel bag drags his shoulder and leg leftward.

"Maybe," Biglar says. "But something tells me we may be pushing too hard on this one."

"Once you cash the quarterly bonus check, you'll forget all about it."

She hears some of what I say, focusing on the view out the back window. "Hey, what do you suppose he is carrying that's so heavy?" Biglar asks.

The hitcher's reflection looms in the passenger side mirror. "Something stolen, no doubt."

3

DESPITE THE TONE of my observations, I am more than a little curious about this man in the rain. I often blow past people like him without thinking. When I'm at the wheel, what matters is my car and the road. Anything that blocks either must go. That I care enough to find him worth my consideration is unusual.

"Where are you headed?" Biglar asks, speaking across me.

The hitcher eyes us.

"Need a ride?" says Biglar. "We're going about thirty miles west."

He grunts, the deep voice pushes out something like a yes. He does not actually say yes, however. This is all the affirmation Biglar wants. She taps the door release with her index finger.

The hitcher's eyes and mine lock for a moment. He follows my glance down to his duffel bag. "Excuse us one second," I say, pressing the window control. Once the electric motor rides the glass back into the seal, I turn to Biglar and say, "Let's get out of here."

"But he needs a ride."

"I didn't hear a yes," I say. "A grunt does not mean yes."

Biglar rolls down my car window again. The air smells of burned oil. Rain drops pelt my worsted wool suit. Beyond the perimeter of the headlights are blackness and water.

I fantasize about pushing Biglar down a long flight of stairs as penance for ignoring me.

4

INSTEAD, I GRIP the wheel with my left hand, jam the gas pedal, and aim for deliverance. Fifteen feet later Biglar regains control of the vehicle when her fist finds my jaw. Clusters of stars cloud my vision. I release the wheel. The brakes squeal as the car jerks to a stop.

"Get in the back," Biglar says. "Or walk." She pushes me clear of the seat and out of the car. Biglar is strong when she's angry. She's kind but very strong. Takes no guff from anyone.

Stepping around the hood, I plop in the backseat and wipe my suit dry on the interior. Another benefit of the twenty-two-dollar-per-day surcharge. We're practically obligated to wreck this car.

The hitcher lays the duffel bag on the road shoulder, climbs inside— into my seat—and buckles up.

"What about your bag?" I ask him.

His voice is deep and scratchy. "You'll get it later."

"Wouldn't it be easier to bring it now?"

"Oh, you'll go back for it." is all the hitcher says.

5

THREE MINUTES LATER, I ask the real question of consequence. "Do you have any money?" I ask. "For gas." A man needs priorities.

Biglar is no help. "The tank is almost full," she says.

"No, not right now," the hitcher says.

"You don't have gas money," I ask, "but you will later?"

"Hap, can we be civil, please?" Biglar tries redirecting the conversation.

"I have your money now," the hitcher says.

6

TRUE, I'M NOT most philosophical man in the world. Some might argue that I'm barely human since my sense of empathy is so skewed. But this business with the hitcher is odd. He could mean a lot of things by his last answer. Then again, maybe he's talking crap; it's just an evasive response. Perhaps he is insane.

Maybe there is no problem here.

Suddenly, he turns in the seat toward me. "What would you do if you lost everything?" the hitcher asks.

"You mean in the stock market?" I ask. "My asset allocation is confidential; but since you bring it up, my strategy is moderately aggressive. I could weather some huge hits and come out all right."

"And what if all your money suddenly belonged to someone else?"

I raise my eyebrows. "Like who?"

The hitcher turns back around and watches me in the passenger side mirror.

7

THE MILES DRIP away slowly, like ice thawing the first day of winter that the temperature rises above the freezing point. My mind keeps returning to the hitcher and his evasiveness. I revert to my earlier impression: He's insane. Shame on Biglar for humoring this irritant.

For her part, Biglar keeps the chatter to a minimum and focuses on the road.

Again the hitcher cracks the silence. "You think money is everything, don't you?" This question hardly sounds like one. "Without it you're nothing."

"That's right," I say. "You may as well not exist."

"And if I have more than you, what does that say about you?"

I laugh. "If someone like you has more than me, I need to figure out what I'm doing wrong. Certainly I make more."

"Do you now?" the hitcher asks.

Oh, how I have him on this one. When traveling, I carry between one and two thousand dollars. Hard currency is like credit and handguns. Better to have both and not need them than to need them and have neither. Fishing in my jacket pocket, I remove a leather wallet. Smells like a tannery in Tuscany, it's so new. I open the main compartment and thumb through the bills, counting.

Almost a thousand in cash, an Amex and a MasterCard check card. Between the three, my reach as a consumer pushes sixty thousand. I could get more funds too if we stop at any ATM or a bank. A phone call to my broker could initiate a wire transfer for an even larger amount. I'm not bragging though.

"You first," the hitcher says.

"Got about a grand." I feel like rubbing his face in it.

"You are certain."

"You want to see it?" I hold up the wallet for Biglar and the hitcher to inspect the contents. "So what do you have?"

The hitcher nods. "That billfold looks expensive."

Biglar glances at me in the rearview mirror. She has a curious expression on her face.

"The finest in Italian craftsmanship. All right, show me yours, Daddy Warbucks," I say.

"Hap?" Biglar says, chuckling.

The hitcher faces forward, saying nothing. I figure he's embarrassed about the size of his stash compared to mine.

"If you can't show me," I say, "then you've got nothing. There's an old saying, Money talks..."

Biglar cuts me off. "You are kidding with us, right?"

"I never joke about fiscal matters," I say.

"There's how much in there?" Biglar asks.

"A thousand. Counted it twice."

Biglar stops laughing. She sounds uncomfortable with what she is about to say. "Hap, you do know your wallet is empty, right?"

8

HER CLAIM IS ponderous. I recount the bills. Nineteen fifties, four twenties, a ten, and some singles. So not quite a thousand, but close enough. I remove the Amex and check for my signature and the security code. Exact same drill with the MasterCard. All there, all right. That Biglar. Thinking I'm kidding. She's sharp when it matters, though some points she misses; this instance must be one of those oversights.

"Maybe I should drive," I say. "Obviously you're exhausted from the flight."

A shake of the head from Biglar. "No."

"I get it," I say. "You two worked up this show in advance. This is one of those let's-bust-on-your-friends things and trick them into questioning their sanity. Maybe they will even believe it for a moment. Okay, game over. You got me." Faking a smile, I flash my teeth. Works great in meetings. Combine it with a firm handshake, and the deal is halfway done. Capped teeth help too.

Biglar though, she knows my tells. But that is not the issue here. For whatever reason, she really thinks I'm destitute.

"I can prove that the money is here." I offer Biglar a receipt from the

ATM. "Read the account balance."

Biglar glances at the slip, turns it over, and clears her throat. "This is blank."

9

I TEAR THE paper out of her hands. The numbers and balances are as I remember them. "Biglar, come on now; I can take a joke, but this is getting retarded. I'm not blind."

"Neither am I," she says. "There's nothing on the paper."

"No one can see your money but you," the hitcher says. "Does that mean you don't exist?"

"You two are the only ones who can't see my money," I say. "Or at least who allege they can't."

The storm kicks up fierce. Street signs sway in the headwinds. Metal rattles. Lightning flashes.

At the strip mall on the right is an ATM machine for a local bank. They probably levy a small fee to check balances, and I'll pay it without flinching. Tonight the charges are worth it to me. I tell Biglar to pull into the lot. She lobbies against me going out in the rain. I convince her anyway.

By the time I reach the ATM, my arms are wet.

I feed my card into the opening. Typing with my first and second fingers, I enter the PIN.

On the display a message reads:

Contact branch manager immediately.

The machine retains my card. A metal wheel on the other side grinds and crushes the plastic to pieces. I curse. Should have stuck with a major chain. I return empty-handed.

Biglar knows from my face how it went; she doesn't ask.

I dial the toll-free number on the back of the Amex. Since cash may not be an option until the bank overnights a new ATM card, better have some credit at my disposal. At the very least, the automated response system can verify my account balance and payment history. That's why I have plenty of both. A mixture of assets is like a twin-turbine plane. May not be the smoothest ride if one engine dies, but as long as the other holds up, it's possible to land in one piece.

The call never connects. On the third try I realize there's no service.

"I need your phone for a minute," I say to Biglar.

"I'm probably out of area too," she says. "We have the same provider."

Her phone works. When the access system prompts for the number, I enter the digits with great care. An automaton voice reads the entry back to me. I verify the number is correct. Instead of the usual voice reciting account details, the call rolls over to another recording: "System does not recognize account number. To open an account, please contact customer service Monday through Friday, 8 a.m. to 5 p.m., Eastern Standard Time."

Before blowing up, I end the call and try again, and punch up the digits. My hand shakes, which is all right. The fingers know exactly where to land.

"System does not recognize account number."

Shutting the clamshell case, I hand back the phone to Biglar.

10

THE WHEELS TURN over the slick pavement. We reach Highway 81. I start counting the dead. Credit card with a nonexistent number, a shredded ATM card, a cell phone out of service for no reason, and cash visible only to myself. And my coworker thinks I'm broke. I've had better Tuesdays.

The fact that the problems began when the hitcher joined the party is not lost on me.

"I didn't catch your name before," I say.

"You wouldn't," says the hitcher.

"My name is Hap."

"You don't know mine because you never care enough to ask people like me."

I collect my thoughts. He's right, in part. "If it was up to me, we probably wouldn't have stopped for you. But all the same, I'd like to know who you are. Can't help noticing a few strange things happened this evening since we picked you up."

"The name is Grant," he says. "Now ask me what happened to your money."

"First off," I say, "I still have my money."

"Do you?"

"Sure. I have this cash for starters." I reach into my wallet again, only now it's empty. No cash, no credit cards. Even the driver's license is missing. "Stop the car, Biglar. We've got a thief on board."

Biglar says, "Hap, I've been right next to him the whole time. I didn't see him take anything from you."

"Then where the hell is it?" I say. "Nothing just disappears by itself."

Biglar slows the car, pulls to the shoulder, and puts the car in park. "I can't drive with this screaming. Let's work this out calmly."

"All right, question one for the thief in the front seat: Did you take my money?" I ask.

"I told you before that I have your money," he says.

"You see!" I say to Biglar. "Better count all your fingers, Biglar. He might have stolen those too. I told you not to stop for him!"

"You lost it all to me before you ever stopped," he says.

"Just give me back my things," I say, "and I'll let you out of the car. You can slink back to wherever you came from in this storm. We won't even bother with the police, because I don't want to waste another second of my life on scum like you."

"It's not here," the hitcher says.

"You threw it out the window?" I say.

"My money is not in the car," the hitcher says.

"No, it's my money! And where is it?" I step out of the car and rip open his door. With one hand, I grab him by the throat and yank him out of the seat. My face is red, my throat scratchy from yelling. "What did you do?"

"What you have done to thousands of others." He speaks between breaths.

"Where is my money?"

Between chokes he smiles. "In the duffel bag."

11

THE RAIN STOPS.

I let go of his neck and let him tumble. He lands on the hood; my fists find his chest and face a few times, until Biglar intervenes. Ever the do-gooder, she knocks me off balance and sends me crashing to the road, knees first. Shock waves hit the pain receptors in my back. I wince.

"Enough!" Biglar says. "Someone is going to get hurt."

"But he robbed me!"

"Hap, come on. Does that make any sense? You never got anywhere near him until right now! You're coming unhinged."

I yell at the hitcher: "Who the hell are you?"

The hitcher leans up on the car, still coughing. "Grant," he says, rubbing his throat. "Grant Tyrell."

"You said Tyrell?" Biglar says.

He nods.

"That's what I wanted to talk to you about," Biglar says to me. "The Tyrell deal."

"The development is named after my grandfather," the hitcher says. "It used to be a farm, but my grandfather sold off pieces to an investment firm. I grew up there."

"So what? This is sacred ground now because Grandpa took a dump out back?" I ask. "You think eminent domain doesn't apply? You think you are going to stop progress?"

"No. Just you."

"What's your address?" I ask. "I'm personally going to run a bulldozer over your place at first light. Your home will be confetti when I'm through."

He laughs, then rises to his feet and starts walking away from us. "It won't take very long if you leave now."

I lunge for him before he can get very far. Biglar cuts between us. "Let him go."

"What?"

"I was worried this might happen," Biglar says. "I knew there was going to be some resistance to this deal. It's just too rich. Sometimes you need to leave more on the table. Even if it doesn't make fiscal sense. It's karma. You finally pushed too hard, and someone is not taking it."

"So I'm successful, and he gets my wallet? What kind of logic is that? Do you always blame victims for the crimes committed against them?"

"I don't know what happened tonight, Hap," Biglar says. "But there just has to be an explanation. Let's go to the hotel and figure it out. Whatever you lost is replaceable."

I know what must be done. "We're going back for the duffel bag."

"I think we're wasting our time," says Biglar. "Neither of you is making any sense."

"I'll drive. And he's coming with us," I say.

Biglar gets in the car. I look for Grant Tyrell. I call his name. But while Biglar and I argued, he must have ducked off into the trees for cover, because I'm the only one on the road.

1 2

BIGLAR'S RENTAL CAR has great acceleration and even better brakes. Good thing, because I drive like hell to reach the bag. Several times Biglar asks me to slow down. I ignore her. She distracts herself by making phone calls, asking questions about Grant Tyrell, the hitcher. All I want is what is mine. If it's in the bag, good. If not, I'll find some other way to settle up. Either way Grant Tyrell will be homeless by dinner. Poor bastard. I almost pity him. Nah.

I lean on the pedal, easing off whenever we reach ninety. Ten minutes later, we are near the spot. Biglar finishes her calls, saying nothing about her findings.

Ahead, the headlights catch the corner of the duffel bag. My attention falls on the road shoulder, where we picked up the hitcher. The bag. The money. My money. So close.

Right before I tap the brakes, Biglar screams.

1 3

IN FRONT OF the car, a man stands with his arms crossed over his chest. A man with a goat tattoo on his neck: Grant Tyrell.

Jamming the brakes hard enough to engage the antilock brake system, I steer toward the wrong side of the road. Even with ABS, we slide. The car fishtails to the left, then right. I steer into the skid. Despite the countermeasure, the rear end swings out anyway; it catches a telephone pole. Inertia takes control. We bounce hard off the pole, spin around, and face the right way, on the other side of the road.

I stop. Biglar is near tears.

"That's not him," I say, mostly for myself.

"It is! I saw him."

Opening the door, I say, "Stay here. I'll check and see if he's okay."

The car is a mess. The rear passenger side is crushed in, exposing most of the tire, which seems bent at an impossible angle. The brake light lamps are busted, the light extinguished. Forget the rear bumper;

that is a disaster. Biglar's twenty-two dollar, no-liability surcharge seems cheap now.

The only part of the car that is intact is the front end. No marks, dents, or blood. Wherever Grant is now, I don't think I hit him. I call his name out as I walk the road and both shoulders. Unlike where I lost him earlier, the terrain is very open, lacking any nooks or crannies in which to disappear.

And yet once again I am alone on the road.

I walk back to the car. Biglar looks even worse.

"I don't see him," I say.

"I think we should leave," Biglar says. "Go to the police."

"If the car still drives," I say. "I'll just pick up what we came out here for."

"No! Don't touch it."

"Why?" I asked, angry, and even more impatient with Biglar.

She sucks in her lips, making them so thin they almost disappear. "Whoever rode in the car with us, it wasn't Grant Tyrell."

"What are you saying?"

"Grant Tyrell died in a car accident on a rainy night four years ago."

14

THE RAIN SLOWS down to a trickle. I walk to the duffel bag. Reaching the right spot, I stand over it for a moment, looking, trying to see what I can. The zipper is partially undone. I must know what is inside.

Kneeling, I pull the zipper the rest of the way.

There are many layers, each one separated with plastic.

In the top layer: one thousand dollars cash, my Amex card, and MasterCard. The number may be right, but the name on the account is Grant Tyrell. Below that are bank account books, checking and savings. My accounts, my balances, in his name. In the next layer are my brokerage statements, IRA statements, and a Roth statement. Right below that are the deeds to my three homes, with the correct addresses, with Grant Tyrell's name listed. According to the documentation, everything of value I own belongs to him.

Footfalls approach me from the rear.

"I told you," Grant Tyrell says, "you'd go back."

"What have you done to me?" I ask.

"You did this. You and your greed. You wanted everything your way.

You drove good people in good neighborhoods onto the streets. You leveled safe communities for shopping malls. You made nothing that the world didn't already have too much of. Now your money will go toward righting the wrongs."

"And what have you ever done in your life that gives you the right to judge me?" I ask.

"Everything I've done is in that bag," he says.

"So that's your contribution to society: you stole my money? What a lovely epitaph."

"There's more in that bag that's precious to you than stocks. Look deeper."

With my hand shaking, I peel away the deeds, revealing another two layers. The first is my driver's license, which, according to the issue date, is expired.

The last layer is unspeakable.

Seeing it, the blood on the duffel bag makes sense.

Wrapped in plastic beneath the documents is a human head; it's mine. Police cars and an ambulance approach in the distance. The sirens whir in the night.

"Without money you are nothing," Grant Tyrell says. In his right hand he holds a machete. "You may as well not exist." As I look into my own dead eyes for the first and last time, I barely feel the cold metal slice cleanly through my neck.

My eyes never change.

SAM HILLIARD lives with his fiancée and four cats in New Jersey. When not toiling at a private boarding school or studying jiujitsu, he is writing the sequel to *The Last Track*. Follow him on twitter @samhilliard or read his blog at: www.samhilliard.com.

Wings

Melanie Cummins

LORA POINTE'S QUIET, horrific murder changed everything I thought I knew about life. Her name sounded surreal, almost like it should be the name of a tropical island; but it was her short, beautiful life that caught the media's attention. With all the sparkle going on in the 1940s, it was incredible that one girl's death brought about so much publicity.

The moment I was legally an adult, I jumped into law enforcement. A girl detective at that time was laughed at, but I pretended not to care. I persevered despite the teasing and the skepticism of my coworkers, driven by my desire to rescue the innocent. My father was captain, but he could only do so much to help calm the pestering of the macho men in my department. It didn't help that my constant companion and sidekick—my dog named Rogue—inspired the squad to give me the charming nickname of Mutt.

The first time they referred to me as "Deputy Mutt," I thought my partner was going to burst, he was laughing so hard. He had a few years on me but was almost as young as I was. We were all babies with guns and badges. My partner, Detective Aaron Gallagher, was a quiet and courageous individual with deep-brown eyes and a rugged smile. He hated that he was stuck with me as a partner. Aaron frequently complained to Captain Willis that he let me "play detective" when I should be a secretary or even a patrol cop. Nonetheless, I respected him; he had pulled me out of more than one perilous situation.

The victim that started this particular mess was actress Lora Pointe. She was twenty when she was murdered. She had been a child actress who had grown into a tall, startling beauty in all the dame movies. She was all kinds of clever—just watching her save the day and get the man of her dreams was inspiring to me.

Three weeks prior, Lora had been found with her green eyes wide-open, her vibrant red hair tangled in knots, her skin so white it was nearly translucent. Her body was settled in a serene position, lying in the middle of a locked and empty room. She had been poisoned, and the squad might have dismissed it to a crazed celebrity stalker; but it happened three more times in the next two weeks. All the women had similar physical features to Lora but were average gals. Lora had been the only famous woman to die. In my spare time I flipped through files, wondering why he chose this certain breed of woman and why he felt the need to kill them.

Aaron walked by, hardly even noticing me, like he always did. I caught the scent of his aftershave and sighed to myself. Aaron would never fancy me the way I fancied him.

"Erika!" Aaron shouted from across the desk. Uh-oh. It was *never* a good thing when he called me by my real first name. He only called me that when he was feeling blue. "Quit daydreamin'!"

Rogue looked up at me, her blue eyes shining. She fancied Aaron as well. Rogue was a present from the captain when I got my badge. She was a Samoyed, a giant, white fluff ball but mean as hell when she wanted to be.

"Sorry, Detective Gallagher," I said.

He glanced at me with a slight twinkle in his eyes. He tried to play mean, but he had a small soft spot for me. It was all *so* confusing at eighteen years old.

The telephone on my desk buzzed. "Hi-de-ho, Deputy Erika Willis," I answered as coolly as possible.

"I poisoned Lora Pointe. I have a tip for you, Miss Willis," the gravelly voice answered. He coughed once, and a chill ran through my body. "Protect the girl on Blue Moon Highway, and I'll give you the next clue."

My entire body had gone cold now. "Who are you?"

My question was answered by a dial tone.

Without consulting anyone or asking permission, I flew the coop. Rogue was at my heels. "Mutt, have you flipped your wig?" Aaron shouted from behind.

"I'm going to Blue Moon Highway!" I yelled back.

I opened the door of my squad car; but honestly, I was directionally challenged and had no idea where to go. Rogue climbed in the passenger seat, smiling at me the way only a dog could.

Aaron appeared at the passenger door, scowling. "Dog, get out." Rogue whined and jumped out, hobbling back to the precinct. "That dog needs to stay home with you. A dog doesn't belong in a police station." When he looked at me again, the soft spot came through. "Where are we going?"

"Oh, quit flapping your lips about Rogue," I replied. "I already answered your question. Blue Moon Highway. I'll explain when we get there."

He walked around the car and shooed me to the passenger side. "I'll drive."

Five minutes later, we were sitting in silence as he drove like a slow poke. "Why, oh why, did I have to get stuck with a bandit like you?" he asked, more to himself than anything.

"Ya know, you really are a grouch. Maybe if you found a woman, you'd be more tolerable. I got a tip, and I'm following it."

"I don't need no woman. We don't need no women in this department either. It's a man's job," Aaron replied. "Get off my back."

I brushed my tangled hair out of my face and blinked away the frustrated tears. No room for crying in law enforcement.

"What did the tip say?"

"Save the girl on Blue Moon Highway," I recited from my sketchy memory. "He said he killed Miss Pointe."

"Oh, Jesus, Mary, and Joseph," cried Aaron. "We get those prank calls all the time." Aaron's face reddened at every word. "Ya know, I'm sick of this. Just because your daddy doesn't want you on the streets as a patrol cop does not mean that you get to ride around with people who actually know what they're doing."

Aaron's tirade was cut off by the whooping of sirens and three patrol cars zooming by us on either side of our slow-moving vehicle. Reacting instantly, he sped up. Our car coughed in return. By the time we caught up with the police cars, they had surrounded a small shack off Blue Moon Highway.

I gave Aaron a look. "Let's go."

Strangely enough, the policemen were swarming around the house and property; but the victim lay alone, crying in the middle of the floor. I dove toward her and pulled her close. She was trembling from head to toe.

Aaron walked up to me with pity in his eyes. "Look at her skin. She's been poisoned. There's nothing we can do. We don't know what the poison is yet, let alone how to counteract it."

I felt sick. I wasn't used to dealing with victims in this position. "I'm

Deputy Erika Willis. What's your name?"

"Rebecca George," she replied. She fit the description: green eyes, fiery-red hair. He had gotten to her, and I hadn't been fast enough to save her.

"Do you remember anything about the person who did this to you?" I asked.

"He told me to tell you to be on the lookout for his next telephone call."

And that was that. Rebecca George passed on without another word. I cradled her close and fought the tears as hard as I could, but they came anyway. She was a baby too, certainly older than I was but maybe only twenty. I felt Aaron's arms wrap around me, pull me up off the ground, and lead me to the squad car. On the ride back to the station, he didn't say a word and or make a joke.

"Stay here," he said when he pulled into the station. Five minutes later, my Rogue was trotting next to Aaron. He opened the backseat of the car and shooed her in.

I looked at him with my eyes full of questions.

"I'm taking you home," he said. "We're done for today."

Aaron knew where I lived because the captain liked to send him over and check on me now and again. It was a little degrading that the captain didn't trust me to be by myself, but I didn't mind the fact that he sent Aaron of all people.

"I hate that he lets you stay by yourself. What kinda father does that?" Aaron muttered to himself.

"I'm not by myself; I have Rogue to protect me."

Rogue lifted her head in the backseat and grinned.

"That mutt is about as good as a pet rat to protect you. She'll snuggle up to the intruder."

We pulled into my apartment driveway. "I'm walking you up," Aaron stated. Rogue and I climbed the stairs first. The sun was beginning to set over our town.

At the door, I thanked Aaron and let Rogue inside. He had an odd look on his face, almost as if he wasn't ready to leave. "You want to come in?" I asked, something fairly inappropriate for a woman my age; but we were friends and partners.

Aaron entered with hesitation but sat himself down on my couch. I wandered around my small apartment, not sure what do with myself. I'd never been alone with Aaron like this before.

"Ma'am, sit down next to me."

I sat.

"I didn't want to go into law enforcement," he said. "I belong in the military. When I got back from the Second World War, it was hard to get out of that mind-set. But I got shot in the leg, and the war ended, and I didn't know what else to do with myself."

"What did you do in the war?"

Aaron *never* talked about the war. It was a sore spot for him. I was curious as to why he was opening up now. "I was in the Army Air Force. My brother and I enlisted together." He pulled out a polished-metal pair of military aviation wings. "We were in the plane together. They kept shooting at us. I don't know how we survived. I honestly don't. We woke up in a hospital together, and I thought it was heaven. I thought God had claimed my soul, but then the pain came. It was real. I was alive."

"Why are you being nice to me today?" I asked. "You're never nice."

He touched the side of my face and followed my jawline down to my chin. "I want you to let me take this case on my own from now on."

"No way," I retorted. "I'm in this now."

"I keep feeling the need to protect you, and I can't. You're more vulnerable as a woman, and I want to take care of this on my own. It has an impact on my own job if I worry about you constantly. I'm turning into a jitterbug."

"I am not more vulnerable, and I'm not getting off this case. Besides, I have to protect you as much as you have to protect me. Men! I can take care of myself."

"You're a stubborn dame," he said, shaking his head.

"Yeah, just like my momma. That's what daddy always says. He knows better than to argue with me, unlike you, Detective Gallagher."

We argued late into the night. We yawned and gradually drifted to sleep on the couch. I woke up an hour later to the sound of a fluttering snore and saw Aaron's body next to mine. I got the strangest feeling in my stomach. And Lord, I don't know what came over me, but I leaned over and placed my lips on his. I had never kissed a man before, but it felt wonderful. I pulled away before I woke him up.

I snuck into my room and crawled into bed. Rogue climbed into bed with me. As I drifted back into sleep, I prayed this wasn't a dream and that he would be there in the morning.

It seemed like a minute later that Rogue slobbered all over my face and woke me up. The sun shone through my curtains, so I groaned and rolled out of bed. When I walked into the living room, I saw a very irritated Aaron Gallagher.

"You're still here," I said, eyes wide-open. "Jesus, Mary, and Joseph, what is the captain going to say about that?"

Aaron walked over to me and leaned in. My heart raced as he touched his lips to my cheek. "He doesn't have to know. Nothing happened." Aaron walked out the door without another word.

The telephone at my house buzzes. "Hi-de-ho," I answered.

"You didn't save her, Erika. You'll have to be punished now."

His voice was so cold that it chilled my body as if I had taken a dip in a frozen pool.

"What's the next clue?" I asked, trying to keep my voice steady.

"Watch *Flapjacks*, and you'll figure it out."

"*Flapjacks*? That's Lora Pointe's movie."

"Now you're cooking with gas."

As soon as I heard the dial tone, I heard a thump and a tumble from outside. I rushed out the door, Rogue at my heels. I screamed as I saw Aaron at the bottom of the steps in a crumpled mess. I rushed to him and lifted his head. He coughed up a little blood.

"Erika, run." He groaned. His eyes widened at something behind me.

I felt a rush of pain through my body as I lost consciousness.

．　．　．

"*WAKE UP, SOLDIER. It's time for your medicine…*"

I could hear Lora Pointe's soft voice in the distance.

"*Yes, you're alive. You'll be out of here in no time. Your family can't wait to see you.*"

I pried open my eyes and saw a flash of her vibrant red hair. I was regaining consciousness, but I still couldn't move. My arms and legs were tied to the chair. I was sitting in my living room with the television flashing in front of me. *Flapjacks*, Lora Pointe's film that made her famous. She was a part-time waitress who volunteered as a nurse for the soldiers returning from the Second World War. It certainly tugged at the heartstrings.

But where was Aaron?

Panic returned, and I fought to get loose. I tried to recall my training, but the adrenaline was clouding my judgment.

Something came over me, and I started screaming at the top of my lungs. A quiet *thump* shut me up. Was the killer still here?

"Oh, Jesus," I whined quietly to myself. I was really done for. The captain would be horrified to find me here, dead, when he had given me the chance to be a rock star detective.

But it was Aaron who came from the hallway, rubbing the bump on his head. The moment he saw me, he rushed over and freed me. "Erika, are you okay?" he asked, frantically searching me for life-threatening wounds.

I wrapped my arms around his shoulders and held on to him as tightly as I could. He had never gotten this close before. It scared me how my feelings grew for him in this moment. I had worked with him for the past eight months and had never told him how I felt. I had silently fallen in love with him. Rogue trotted out from the bedroom, looking sullen as well. When she woofed, we pulled apart.

"Come on, Willis, we gotta catch this guy," Aaron said.

We drove slowly back to the station. I was more than frazzled, but Aaron seemed in control of himself. "What did you see?" I asked.

"A masked man pushed me down the stairs. I saw him clobber you over the head and drag you up the stairs. I woke up in your bed." Those facts were laid down in a matter-of-fact way. He was smothering his fear.

"I thought you were dead."

"Nah, obviously I'm invincible." He attempted a smile.

"Why did he want me to watch *Flapjacks*?" I asked. "What kind of crazy, pathetic killer wants me to watch a motion picture?"

Aaron didn't respond, and our conversation faded.

• • •

I WATCHED FROM outside the captain's office as Aaron updated him on our situation. The more Aaron spoke, the redder the captain's face became and the louder he words came out.

Aaron came out and slammed the door behind him. "We think we know why he killed Lora Pointe," he said. "He might have been in the Second World War. Something about a redheaded nurse got to him. Maybe he was in extraordinary pain and saw the film or had a nurse who had those features."

"Either way, I want you both off this case. I've already handed the case over to another detective," boomed the captain from his office. "No arguing. You yucks need to take some time off."

Aaron shrugged and sat down at his desk across from mine. I held my head in my hands and sighed to myself. So close…

"Come on, Mutt, cheer up."

"My name is Deputy Erika Willis, thank you very much!"

The entire building grew silent. Aaron raised his eyebrow at me.

"I know I'm a woman, and you think I should be washing the dishes; but I am a police officer, and I help people. I demand some respect! Get over yourself and let me do my job without being *humiliated*!"

Someone whispered, "Uh-oh, Mutt's snapped her cap."

"I thought she fancied Gallagher," the other whispered back. "Why is she yelling at him like that?"

I ran to the stalls, red-faced that had I opened my mouth in the first place. I would never be the ace detective who could attract a man like Aaron Gallagher. I was nothing but a loser.

I trotted out later after I had calmed down. Thankfully, no one looked at me or said a word. I slumped down at my desk and avoided Aaron's glances.

The phone buzzed.

"Deputy Willis," I answered with a sigh.

"Hey, honey." It was *his* voice. "Where do you go to find my next victim?"

"You tell me," I said.

"The warehouses on Dolly Lane. Go now. You and I need to talk to each other in person."

Without consulting Aaron, or anyone in the station for that matter, I flew out the door. I could do this alone.

• • •

THE WAREHOUSES ON Dolly Lane were a hangout for hoodlums who amuzed themselves by vandalizing them. Transients loved to live in the abandoned buildings. The warehouses were one of the most feared places to enter in the area, simply because of their dark and expansive interiors.

I slid the door open. A couple of birds squawked and flew past my head.

He was in the shadows, decked out in black from head to toe.

"Where is she?" I asked.

"She's right there," he said, lifting his gun to me. "Deputy Erika Willis."

"I'm not your type," I said. "Brown hair, blue eyes. Not your type."

"You're my brother's type. You're a distraction for him." The man charged closer to me. I saw a bottle of blue liquid tied around his neck. "I have a gift for you. Take it, and I won't kill Detective Gallagher." He shifted the range of his gun to the left, to something behind me.

"Come on, David, put down the gun." I heard the tense voice of Aaron. "I don't want to shoot you."

"You won't shoot me, brother."

I could feel Aaron's presence move closer. "We fought in the war together. We survived together. Quit the games. You're better than this."

"We woke up in that hospital. I wanted to die. I should have died. And that redheaded nurse kept me alive," David said. "Those green eyes kept me alive through the torment."

Aaron looked defeated. "Why keep killing?"

"Killing takes the pain and the nightmares away." David gazed at me, blue eyes shining. "Take the poison, star detective, and save the man you love. If you don't, you both will die."

I held out my hand, and he placed the bottle of blue liquid in my palm. I looked back at Aaron with tears in my eyes. "I love you, Detective Aaron Gallagher," I whispered. I closed my eyes and slugged back the contents that would take my life.

Aaron lifted his gun and aimed for David's head, but David was faster. He shot Aaron in his already injured leg, causing him to fall to the ground. The gun was pointed at me now, but David's hands were trembling. I wasn't his type. My death was harder than the others.

I moved quicker than I knew I could, and I snatched up Aaron's gun, pointed, and shot. With one hit, David dropped to the floor. I crawled over and took his gun away. He clutched his military aviation wings in both his hands. He whispered the name of the poison, and he took his last breath staring into my eyes.

I lifted up Aaron with what was left of my strength, and we hobbled into the sunshine. A dozen or so squad cars were waiting outside. The captain was first in line. He had a mix of emotions on his face.

"She needs to get to the hospital," Aaron said. "She was given the poison that killed the others."

After I told them the name of my poison, I was out cold.

• • •

I WOKE UP with a splitting headache and a warm hand clutching mine. Aaron was asleep in the chair next to my hospital bed. He stirred as I stroked his dark hair.

"I told them no nurses," he said. "I figured we had enough of those in all this jazz."

"I'm sorry about your brother."

Aaron shook his head. "I had my suspicions when he made you watch *Flapjacks*. He was obsessed with that movie for months after getting out of the hospital. I just didn't want to believe that my brother was capable of those murders."

"How did you know to go to the warehouse?"

"I'm pretty good at tracking my favorite female detective," Aaron said. He leaned over and pressed his lips on mine. When he pulled away, he had a soft smile on his mouth. "Can I take you out on a date, Miss Willis?"

I was twitterpated for Aaron Gallagher.

Interrupting the love spell, the captain walked in with a grimace. "Congratulations, Detective Erika Willis."

"Detective?" I asked.

Aaron grinned at me. "Yes, ma'am. No more harassment. We had a talk with the other men in the department. After I told them what a gunslinger you are, they aren't going to mess with ya."

"But the mutt has to stay at your apartment," The captain said. "That thing is too girly. We gotta keep up our image, ya know? Maybe I'll get you a bulldog for graduating to detective." He walked out of the room before I could argue back.

The tiny television hummed words at us. I recognized Lora Pointe's film, *Lovers Lane,* and grew sad at her lost life.

"So, what do you say? Can I take you out sometime?"

"I would love to go on a date with you, Detective Gallagher," I replied.

The hospital telephone rang beside my bed. "It's probably the deputies checking on us," Aaron said, noticing how tense I became at the sound. "My brother is dead, so quit worrying."

He picked up the phone. After a few seconds, I glanced at him and saw that the blood had drained out of his face.

"David?" he whispered into the phone. "Brother, is that you?"

MELANIE CUMMINS is a criminal justice student at the University of West Florida. She has been published in *Mystery Times Ten 2011*. She hopes to be a detective one day and write about her adventures.

Trapped

Donna Jean McDunn

STACIE ADAMS IMPATIENTLY drummed her fingers on the desk. Jeff would be expecting her to run. She should never have asked him for help. The bell sounded, and Stacie was out of the classroom and on her way to the front doors by the time the bell had stopped.

She ignored the cold rain. Nothing was going to stop her from finding Julie. She turned the corner and ran smack-dab into Kyle Evans.

"Whoa, slow down, Stacie. What's your hurry?"

He'd caught her by the shoulders. She stared into his blue eyes, and something inside her turned to mush. Great! She finally gets Kyle to notice her, and Jeff is hot on her trail. She tore her eyes away long enough to glance over her shoulder to see if Jeff was following. She didn't see him. Relieved, she turned back to Kyle.

He still held her by the shoulders. "Sorry, Kyle. I've gotta go." She tried to step around him. He tightened his grip.

"Hey, that hurts. You…"

Kyle suddenly released her.

She rubbed her shoulders where his fingers had dug in. She gave him a dirty look. "What was that for?"

"We need to talk, Stacie," Jeff said. "Thanks, Kyle."

She frowned at Jeff. He was smiling. She frowned at Kyle. He wouldn't meet her gaze. "Oh, now I get it. You were waiting for me." Boys couldn't be trusted. They run in packs like dogs. Maybe she should rethink having a crush on her brother's best friend.

"I knew you'd bolt," Jeff said. "I figured you'd be heading for the bus stop."

Stacie's face grew warm; her hands clenched into fists. "I have to go, Jeff. Don't you understand? Julie's trapped somewhere."

Jeff's eyes filled with pain. "Stacie, no one wishes more than I do that Julie is alive, but she's gone. The tornado ripped the diner apart. No one else survived. It's been a week, and even if she'd survived the tornado…" His voice cracked, and he let his words trail off.

She wanted to scream at him, "Julie's not dead! Not yet!" But he already thought she was losing it, and that would only add fuel to the fire. She took a deep breath and repeated, in a calm voice, what she'd told him that morning. "Julie was not in the diner when the tornado struck. She was taken before it happened. I saw her."

"Here we go again, *seeing* things," Jeff interrupted. "You can't be serious?"

"She's my twin sister. I would know if she was dead. She needs my help."

"Julie's alive?" Kyle interrupted.

Startled, because she'd forgotten he was there. Her stomach flipped. Well, that probably ended any hope she'd ever had of Kyle liking her. Now he'll think she's nuts too.

Jeff was quick to answer him. "Stacie *thinks* Julie is alive."

Stacie stomped her foot. "I know she is. I've seen her."

Jeff sighed, rubbed his forehead, and rolled his eyes. "Stacie thinks she's psychic."

"How do you know she isn't?" Kyle asked.

Stacie's mouth dropped open.

Jeff was the first to recover. "You believe in that stuff?"

Kyle shrugged. "I like to keep an open mind. I've never known anyone who was psychic, but that doesn't mean it doesn't exist. I've never met any astronauts either."

Jeff's shoulders slumped. "Okay, I give up; if I can't talk you out of it, then I'll have to take you." Jeff ran his hand through his hair. "So, where do we start?"

It had taken him long enough to come around. That was all she'd wanted in the first place. "There's a dirt road that crosses some railroad tracks behind a grain elevator. She's being held in some sort of building in the woods. She's alone right now, but I don't know for how long."

"Do you know who took her?" Kyle asked.

She studied his face. Did he really believe her, or was this just another ploy to make his friend's little sister look stupid? "No, I don't know his name, and I couldn't see his face."

"Did you see anything else?" he asked.

Kyle didn't smile or look smug, unlike her brother, who thought she was nuts. Maybe Kyle was sincere and really wanted to know what she'd seen in the vision. "I saw a man driving a red truck. You know, like a semitractor-trailer."

"Oh, that narrows it down," Jeff said. "Do you at least know what town this grain elevator is in?"

"No, but I'll know it when I see it."

Jeff shook his head and sighed. "Okay, let's go. Kyle, are you coming?"

"Sure, when you find Julie, you guys might need my help."

Maybe she'd misjudged Kyle?

• • •

STACIE SAT IN the backseat. She wasn't very happy with her big brother right now. Jeff kept making sarcastic remarks. He'd already said he thought they'd driven far enough and should go home.

Kyle twisted around so he could see Stacie. "So how long have you been psychic?"

Stacie grinned. "I was five the first time." She leaned forward as far as her seatbelt would let her. "Jeff was seven. Julie and I were playing in our room when suddenly I thought I was outside. I looked up in the tree, and Jeff was dangling from a tree branch. His hands slipped, and he fell to the ground. His arm was bent at a strange angle."

"Jeff broke his arm when he was seven?" Kyle asked.

"No, I did not," Jeff said. "I don't know what she thinks she remembers, but that didn't happen."

"I never said you broke your arm. I said I saw you break it in the vision; but when I told Julie what I saw, we ran outside, and sure enough, there was Jeff clinging to a tree branch. We found an aluminum ladder of Dad's and propped it up so Jeff could climb down." She took a deep breath. "Do you remember that, Jeff?"

"Sure, and I told you I didn't need your help. I could get down anytime I wanted."

Stacie grinned at Kyle. "Yeah, he did say that, but he used the ladder. When he was on the ground, I told him what I saw happen in the vision. He got all mad and everything and said I had ruined his fun and that I was nuts. After that I was afraid to tell anyone about the visions, except Julie, of course."

Kyle laughed. "I'd say he's still in denial."

Stacie grinned.

Jeff tapped Kyle on the arm. "You two quit talking about me like I'm not here." He looked into the rearview mirror at Stacie. "So far we've been to five different grain elevators. How long are you going to pretend you know what you're looking for?"

Stacie leaned back against the seat. "We can't give up until we find Julie or run out of places to look."

Jeff shook his head. "The car is almost out of gas. I'm heading home."

He couldn't do this, not now when they were so close. "Jeff, you can't. We can get more gas."

"I don't have any money," Jeff said. "Do you? How far are these grain elevators? We've already been to every town within a fifty-mile radius. We're a long way from home." He stopped on the side of the road and turned to look at her. "Do you want to walk back? Or worse, call Mom and Dad to come and get us. Besides, if we don't get home soon, they're going to start to worry. Don't you think they've been through enough, losing a daughter and a business?"

"I've already taken care of Mom and Dad. It's Friday night. I told them we were spending the night with friends. Look, Jeff, I have some babysitting money I've been saving. You can have it all." She tossed the money onto Jeff's lap. "There's a couple of hundred there."

Jeff glanced at Kyle. "What about you? Do you need to go home?"

Kyle shook his head. "Nah, my parents think I'm spending the night at your house."

Jeff picked up the money and stuffed it into his jacket pocket. "All right, I'll stop for gas; but as soon as we've checked these places, we go home."

· · ·

STACIE MARKED THE elevator they just left off the list—two more after this one and then what? She refused to quit looking for Julie as long as she could feel her waiting for them. She's cold and scared, but she's alive.

Jeff stopped the car beside the next grain elevator. Stacie got out of the car and looked around just as she had at all the rest. It looked pretty much like all the others until she noticed the muddy road that disappeared among the trees on the edge of the property. This was it.

Stacie's heart beat faster as she got back in the car. "The road is on the other side of the railroad tracks." She pointed. "We have to get back there."

Jeff crossed over the railroad tracks and stopped. "It's mud. I can't drive on that. We'll get stuck."

Stacie slung the backpack onto her shoulder and opened the car door. "Then we'll walk." She waited by the side of the car for Jeff and Kyle. They looked at each other and then at her. They weren't coming. She shrugged, hefted the backpack onto her back, and walked away. She heard the car doors open and close but didn't look back.

Jeff caught her arm. "Look, Stacie, I'm not saying your wrong; but it's dark. We should come back tomorrow when it's daylight."

Stacie yanked her arm free from Jeff's grip and never missed a step. "Julie doesn't have until tomorrow. I brought flashlights; they're in my backpack."

Jeff sighed. "I should have known."

Stacie rummaged around in the bag as she walked. She found the flashlights and tossed him one. She glanced at Kyle. "I only brought two. I guess we'll have to share."

Kyle shrugged. "I don't mind."

The mud clung to their shoes. Walking was slow and tedious. Stacie's legs ached before they had gone twenty feet.

Jeff was having the same problem. "This is crazy. How much farther?"

The truth was, she didn't know. "We're getting closer. We have to hurry. He'll be coming back."

"How do you know?" Jeff asked.

Stacie didn't answer. How could she explain a feeling? She could call it a premonition, but that would send Jeff over the edge. She walked faster but then stopped when the road suddenly split and went in opposite directions. Both roads were equally muddy, with the same deep ruts. Which way was the right way? And did it even matter? Stacie didn't know, but she wasn't about to tell Jeff. He'd quit for sure and maybe his friend would too. Kyle hadn't said anything since they'd started down the muddy road, but the frown on his face told her he wasn't happy.

Jeff caught up with her. He picked up a stick and tried to scrape the mud off his shoes. "Oh, this is great. What are we doing out here? It's cold, dark, and this mud…it won't come off. My feet feel like they weigh a ton." He kicked his foot, trying to shake the mud loose.

"I'm not giving up, Jeff. You and Kyle can leave if you want to. But I know Julie is somewhere out here, and I'm not leaving without her."

Jeff stopped kicking and stared at her. "Stacie, she couldn't be out here. The tornado didn't come this way."

"Jeff," she said as if talking to a very small child. "How many times do I have to say it? The...tornado...didn't...take...Julie." Her voice grew louder with each word. "Some trucker dude in a red semi took her. He has her trapped out here, and I'm going to find her BEFORE he gets back tonight, with or without your help."

Jeff stared at her. "Okay, calm down. I get it. Which way do we go?"

"This way." She took the closest route and trudged through the mud.

Stacie shined her flashlight into the woods, hoping to get a glimpse of a building. The rain had stopped, but a light fog had settled in. All the sounds they made were magnified as it echoed around them in the fog. It was eerie.

Jeff suddenly stopped dead in his tracks. "I don't believe it. Stacie! Look!"

Stacie's eyes followed the beam of light. Hidden in the brush was the outline of a building.

"It has to be it, right, Stacie?" Jeff asked.

"I don't know," she answered. "I have to get closer."

The three of them made their way through the tangle of trees and brush. The building was made of old, weathered wood and wasn't much bigger than a closet. There weren't any windows except an opening along the top above the missing door.

Stacie shook her head. "This isn't it. It's an old outhouse. But the house is close by."

Jeff slapped the palm of his hand with the flashlight. "How do you know? You didn't even look inside."

"I don't need to. I..." Pain shot through her temple. It was a bad one. It was the worst "vision" pain she'd ever felt. It must be because she was so close. She grabbed the side of her head and bent over.

She felt Jeff put his arm around her. "Stacie, what's wrong?"

"What happened? Is she all right?" Kyle asked.

She heard them but couldn't answer. Her heart was beating so loud, she feared it might explode. Then the pain was gone, and she could no longer hear Kyle and Jeff. She felt as if she was slipping away from them.

Was she dying? She wondered where she was going. Would Julie be there? Then she could "see" it. A tiny cabin surrounded by trees and brush. A man climbed out of a red semi and entered a path that led to the back door of a boarded-up cabin. He was whistling. He easily pulled the boards off. Then the vision was gone.

She was a little disoriented until she heard Jeff's voice. "We'll have to carry her," he was saying. "You get her feet."

Stacie felt her legs being lifted. Jeff and Kyle were going to carry her out of the woods before she had a chance to rescue Julie. She kicked and twisted her body. She wasn't going anywhere. Kyle let go of her legs, and she plopped onto the muddy road.

Jeff gasped. "Why'd you drop her?"

"She kicked me in the nose." Kyle's voice sounded strange.

Stacie struggled to get out of the sticky mud. She still held the flashlight. She pointed it toward Kyle's voice. He had his hand over his nose. Blood dripped between his fingers. She sucked in a sharp breath. "Kyle, I'm sorry."

He held up his hand. "It's okay. Don't worry about it."

He didn't sound okay. He probably hated her now. She'd have to worry about that later. Right now she had to find the cabin where Julie was being held prisoner.

Jeff put his arm around her. "Come on, Stacie. Let's get out of here."

Stacie pulled away from him. "No, I'm staying. I saw the cabin. It's close by. You and Kyle can go if you want."

She went past the outhouse and into a thicket of tangled trees and brush. She ignored the sharp thorns that tore at her clothes. If they ripped her skin, she didn't notice.

"Stacie, wait," Jeff said.

She pointed the flashlight in the direction of his voice. Kyle and Jeff had followed her.

"Are you crazy?" Jeff asked. His hands were lifted above the thorny bushes. "Slow down or these thorns are going to rip you to pieces."

"I can't slow down. I have to get there before he does."

She heard him mumble something about crazy little sisters.

She pushed her way through the thick growth and finally stumbled into a clearing of sorts. The grass and weeds were as tall as she; but the thorny trees were gone, and the cabin she'd seen in the vision was in the middle of it.

Jeff and Kyle came stumbling into the clearing behind her.

"This better be it," Jeff said.

Stacie nodded. "It is."

Jeff examined the house. "So this is what you saw when you freaked out back there?"

Stacie frowned. "I didn't freak out. I had a vision."

He ignored what she said. "It's not much of a building." He knocked on the weathered plywood covering the door. "It's all boarded up. It looks like it's been this way for years."

"It's more of a building than that outhouse," Kyle said. "And you wanted her to examine that."

Stacie snorted. She couldn't help it. Kyle had defended her to Jeff, his best friend. Maybe he wasn't mad about the kick in the nose after all.

"Come on. There's a path on the other side of the house that leads to the back door," she said. "That's the door he's been using."

"Someone's definitely been here," Kyle said. "The path is worn."

"Yeah," Jeff said, "but this door's boarded up too."

Stacie sighed. "These are new boards. The ones on the other door are old and weathered. Why do you suppose someone would bother to put new boards on this old place if they weren't hiding something?" She pulled on the board but couldn't move it. "Help me pull these off."

Jeff pushed her away from the door. "Stacie, are you crazy! That's breaking and entering."

She looked up at him. "Yeah, I know. Are you going to help? If not, get out of my way." She stepped around him. Kyle joined her. Jeff watched for a few seconds, sighed, and joined in.

As soon as they were inside, Jeff stood in the middle, sweeping his arms in a dramatic arc. "The place is empty. Now can we go home?"

Stacie stood beside Kyle. "No, she's here. Don't you hear that?"

"Hear what?" Jeff asked. "Oh…maybe, I'm not sure."

"Over here, Jeff, listen," Kyle said. "It's *tap, tap, tap.* Do you hear it?" Kyle looked down at the floor. "It's coming from right here."

Jeff stood beside Kyle. "Yeah, you're right."

Stacie dropped to her knees. She tapped on the floor and waited. A few seconds later she heard an answering tap. She pushed on the floor. It seemed solid.

"There must be a way in. Step away; maybe you're standing on it." She pushed on the floor again, and part of it slid to the side.

Jeff sucked in a sharp breath. "Oh! My…Stacie I'm so…Julie…I don't believe this."

"Jeff, it's okay. I know it's a shock, but don't just stand there blubbering; use your cell, call 911. Tell them to hurry. There's not much time. He'll be back soon."

Stacie helped Julie sit up. She pulled off the blindfold and carefully removed the duct tape from her mouth.

"I don't have a signal." Jeff turned in different directions. "All these trees must be interfering."

"Get me out of this hole." Julie's voice was hoarse. She clung to Stacie's hand. "He put me in here a few days ago. He came back a couple of times and gave me water and said he'd be back to play later, but I knew you would find me first." She began to cry softly.

Stacie took off her backpack. Opening it, she brought out a bottle of water. "You're safe now. Here, drink this." Julie gulped some water. Stacie took the bottle from her. "That's enough for now. It might make you sick. We have to get you out of here."

She looked at her brother. "Jeff, run to the dirt road; maybe you can get a signal there. If not, go back to the car and keep going until you do. Kyle can help me with Julie. If the creep shows up before we get out of here, we'll hide in the woods. Now go."

To her amazement Jeff didn't argue. He hugged her and whispered into her ear, "I'll never doubt you again, little sis, and thanks for saving my arm."

He grasped her hand and shoved something into it, and then he was gone. Stacie wrapped her fingers around the object. It was the rest of her babysitting money.

She stuffed the money into her pocket. "Julie, do you think you can walk?

"I don't know, but I'll try," Julie said.

"Kyle, can you help me? We may have to carry her."

Kyle nodded. "Sure, what do you want me to do?"

Stacie motioned for him to move to Julie's other side. She and Kyle held her between them and carried her outside. "The path is the quickest way to the dirt road. It isn't far. He parks his truck and walks back here, so we have to hurry."

"Hey, guys, I need to sit down," Julie said. "I feel…" Julie suddenly became very heavy as she sank into their arms.

"Is she all right?" Kyle asked.

"I think she fainted." Stacie looked at Kyle. "I don't think we'll be able to carry her out of here in time."

He picked up Julie. "Then we hide in the woods like you told Jeff."

Kyle carried Julie to the base of a large oak tree with plenty of thorny bushes and vines for them to hide behind. Julie was still unconscious, but she was breathing.

Stacie held the flashlight out to Kyle. "Hold this, please?"

Kyle took the light, and Stacie opened the backpack and found a hooded sweatshirt. "Set that on the ground and hold Julie up while I put these on her? I didn't want to take the time to put these on her back at the cabin."

"Sure," he said. "You really came prepared, didn't you?"

She shrugged. "I had too. No one would listen to me." She slipped the black sweater over Julie's head. "I knew Julie was wearing a white uniform. It isn't very warm and makes a lousy outfit to hide in." She found the matching sweatpants and slipped them onto Julie's legs. Kyle lifted her so Stacie could pull them up.

She examined Julie's face; she appeared to be sleeping. "I hope she's okay. I wish she'd wake up so I could ask her."

Kyle reached across Julie and took Stacie's hand and squeezed it. "She's going to be fine…now."

Stacie smiled into his eyes. "I'm glad you're here, Kyle."

His eyes lit up. He squeezed her hand again. "Yeah, me too."

He leaned toward her. "Do you think…I mean, sometime…would you…?" He stopped and looked around. "Do you hear that?"

Stacie held her breath. What had he been about to ask? She hadn't heard anything. "Kyle, what…" Then she heard it too, the unmistakable rumble of a diesel engine. She gripped his free hand. "Turn off the flashlight."

Kyle turned off the light only seconds before headlights shone through the trees and blinded them. The engine stopped, and they were plunged back into darkness. The truck door slammed. Julie moaned.

Stacie's stomach churned. "Oh, not now, Julie."

She could hear him whistling. Stacie hugged Julie to her. Would the guy try and find them once he realized Julie was gone?

Stacie jumped when he yelled, "No!" She recognized the next sound as the trapdoor being slammed shut. Then there were running footsteps going back in the same direction he had come. The diesel engine roared to life, and they were flooded in light again.

"He's getting away," Stacie whispered. "He's getting away, Kyle. We need to stop him."

"Don't worry about it," Jeff said. "I think the cops can handle things from here."

Stacie jumped to her feet. "Jeff! How did you find us?" She hugged him.

"I came in here to hide when that creep drove in. I saw you in the headlights, but I couldn't say anything until he left. How's Julie."

"I'm all right," Julie whispered. "Thanks to you three."

Jeff knelt down beside her and held her hand. "The cops are waiting by the train tracks. They didn't want to alert him, so they came with no sirens or flashing lights." His eyes met Stacie's. "They'll send the ambulance in as soon as they have him in custody. I should have listened to you."

"It's okay, you're listening now."

Kyle held Stacie's hand. Jeff looked from her to Kyle. His eyebrows rose. "So what's been going on? Is there something we need to talk about?"

• • •

STACIE JUMPED UP from the couch. "What do you mean, 'they had to let him go'? Jason Andrews kidnapped our sister." She shuddered. "How could they do that?"

Jeff sat on the recliner and put his face in his hands. "There wasn't enough evidence to hold him." He looked up. "Where are Mom and Dad? We need to tell them right away before they hear it on the news."

Stacie flopped back onto the couch. "They're at the hospital. The doctors released Julie this morning." Tears burned in her throat. "It's only been two days. Mom and Dad are going to be so upset, and Julie...I can't even imagine how this will affect her."

Jeff shook his head. "It's going to be rough, but we'll manage. We've been through worse. At least we know what we're up against." He tried to smile. "Hey, I'm surprised you didn't go to the hospital."

"I wanted to, but I stayed home to…Oh, my gosh! I forgot Julie's cake in the oven." Stacie bolted for the kitchen.

The oven timer went off just as she opened the oven door. Relieved, she set the cake on a cooling rack and mixed up the frosting.

"Jeff," she called from the kitchen. "I have to let Julie's cake cool. Would you help me hang the 'welcome home' banner?"

Jeff didn't answer. She went to the living room. Out of the corner of her eye she saw movement through the bay window. Why would Jeff be outside?

"Stacie, did you want me?" Jeff asked from the top of the stairs.

Startled, Stacie gasped. "Jeff, I could have sworn you were standing by the window just now."

He shook his head. "It wasn't me. I've been in my room." He came down the stairs and looked out the window. "What did you see?"

She shrugged. "Nothing really, just a shadow. It could have been a passing car."

He glanced out the window again. "I know who you saw. You need to tell your boyfriend to stop being a Peeping Tom."

She felt her face grow warm. Of course, she'd forgotten about inviting Kyle over for the party. The doorbell rang. "I'll get it, and he's not my boyfriend…yet."

• • •

STACIE JUMPED OFF the ladder and admired their work. "Jeff, Kyle, what do you think? How's the banner look?"

Kyle grinned. "I think we finished just in time. Your mom and dad just drove in."

Stacie took a deep breath. She wasn't sure she was up to this, but she didn't want to ruin Julie's homecoming; the bad news could wait until later.

She rushed outside to greet her sister. Her dad already had the video camera running. Grabbing Julie in a big bear hug, she said, "I'm so glad you're home."

"Me too," Julie said. "Thanks to you."

Stepping back, Stacie held Julie at arm's length. "You'll never guess. I've baked you a surprise."

Julie's eyes widened. "No way! You baking? I don't believe it."

Stacie nodded. "Well, believe it. Nothing is too much trouble for you, little sister."

Julie laughed. "Oh, come on!" She rolled her eyes. "You're only three minutes older than me."

It was good to see Julie laugh. Stacie put her arm around her waist and drew her toward the door. "I know, but that three minutes still makes you the little sister."

Jeff waited on the front porch, grinning. He stepped in front of them, blocking the steps. He opened his arms wide. "You're both little sisters, and big brother wants a hug too."

Once inside, Stacie stayed close to Julie, watching her smile and joke with Jeff and Kyle. She sounded and acted like her old self, the social butterfly; but Stacie wasn't fooled. She could see the fear and anger Julie was trying so hard to hide from everyone. How could she tell her Jason Andrews was a free man?

"I love the banner," Julie said. "So what's my surprise?"

"Your favorite," Stacie said. "Chocolate cake. I need to frost it yet."

"Good." Their mom slipped an arm around each girl. "I'm declaring this family night. Let's all go into the kitchen and watch."

Stacie glanced around the table as she frosted the cake. Her heart felt as though it might burst. She'd never thought much about what her family meant to her until Julie went missing. She had taken them all for granted.

She smiled at Kyle. He smiled back. She looked down at the cake. He'd been watching her all evening. He hadn't resumed the conversation he'd begun in the woods. Maybe he'd had a change of heart and didn't know how to tell her.

Her dad cleared his throat. "I have some news you'll all want to hear. I talked to the insurance company. They said the insurance will cover most of the cost of rebuilding the diner."

Jeff grinned. "That's great news, Dad. How soon do you think we can start building?"

Dad smiled. "Probably by the end of the month."

Jeff's grin included Julie. "Hear that, Julie? You and I will soon have our jobs back. For a while there, I thought we might have to take up babysitting."

Julie's smile disappeared. She clutched the edge of the table, her body visibly shaking. The fear and anger Stacie had seen inside her were suddenly very visible to everyone.

Mom came around the table and kneeled down on the floor beside her. "Julie, honey, what's wrong?"

Julie shook her head. She looked up with wide, frightened eyes. Tears slid down her cheeks. "I...I...I'm sorry, Mom. I can't go back there. Not after..."

Mom's eyes filled with tears. She wrapped Julie in her arms. "Don't worry about that. We aren't going to make you do anything you don't want to do. It'll be months before the diner is finished anyway, and if you still don't want to come back...well...we'll figure something out then."

Stacy pushed the frosted cake to the middle of the table. It wasn't the best time to tell them about Jason Andrews, but there never would be a good time.

Jeff must have been thinking the same thing. He stood and cleared his throat. All eyes turned to him. "I hate to ruin the party, but I have to tell you something. There's no easy way to say this, so I'll just say it. Jason Andrews has been released."

"How is that possible?" Dad asked. "He was caught red-handed."

Jeff shook his head. "The police say there's no concrete evidence. They said the only fingerprints they found were ours and a few smudged ones that weren't any good. Julie wasn't...you know, hurt, so there's no DNA evidence. The fact he was there wasn't all that unusual. Truckers from the grain elevator use the road to turn around because it makes a big loop, and he claims he never went inside the building."

"Julie identified him as her kidnapper," Mom said.

Jeff shook his head. "He kept her blindfolded. She's not 100 percent positive. She never saw his face. She recognized his voice as belonging to someone she'd talked to at the diner. The DA says that's not enough for a conviction."

"But Julie knew him. She said he came there all the time. She said he gave her the creeps." Her mom was visibly shaking.

"Lots of people give me the creeps, and lots of truckers go to the diner. That doesn't make them the kidnapper." Jeff took a deep breath. "Look, I said the same things to the cops. They said all the evidence was circumstantial, and there's nothing the police can do without hard evidence. They said if they go to court with what they have on him, he'd probably get off anyway."

• • •

THE BAD NEWS ruined the party just as Stacie had thought it would. Julie ran upstairs, and Kyle and Jeff claimed the TV to watch a football game. Stacie volunteered to clean up the kitchen so Mom and Dad could be near Julie.

She welcomed the time alone to think. There had to be something they could do to put Jason Andrews behind bars.

She rinsed the dishes and stacked them in the dishwasher. She had just put the last glass into the machine when it happened. The pain came suddenly like before, trying to split her head in two, and was gone just as suddenly.

She was outside; the only light came from the streetlight on the corner. The hair on her arms stood up, and she knew he was watching her. She lifted the lid of the metal trash can and dropped the bag inside. She didn't feel any fear, only a little apprehension as she waited for him to make a move.

Jason Andrews grabbed her from behind. He was holding a knife. "I've been waiting for you, Julie."

"Stacie, can you hear me? What's wrong? Stacie…"

Like the vision she'd had in the woods, she could hear Jeff and Kyle talking, but she couldn't answer right away. She sucked in a deep breath and choked, but she forced out the words. She grabbed Jeff's arm. "He thinks I'm Julie. That's how we can get him."

Jeff pulled his arm free and rubbed it. "What are you talking about?"

"That shadow I saw by the window." She looked at Kyle. "Tell him you didn't look in the window before you came to the door."

"No, I…"

"See, I told you," Stacie interrupted. "It was Andrews, and he doesn't know Julie has a twin sister. I didn't work at the diner. He'll think he's getting Julie, but it will be me." The more she thought about it, the more excited she became. "Don't you see? We can record it all with Dad's camera. The police need proof. How much more could they need than a confession from the kidnapper?"

Jeff and Kyle were already shaking their heads. "Stacie, are you crazy?" Jeff asked.

She lifted her chin. "Will you stop asking me that? Something has to be done about Jason Andrews. Who better than the three of us?"

He was still shaking his head.

She turned to Kyle. "You'll help me, won't you?"

A look of pain crossed his face. "I want that animal put away too, but I'm with Jeff on this one."

"How can either of you say no when you haven't heard the plan?"

Jeff sat down at the kitchen table. "Okay, let's hear it, if it'll make you feel better. Then I'll say no."

Stacie sank into a chair across from Jeff. She smiled at Kyle when he sat beside her and clasped her hand under the table. She took a deep breath and told them what she'd seen in the vision. She didn't mention the knife. "So you see, if we can record him saying those words while he thinks he has kidnapped Julie, we can put him away for life. All we need is the police ready to arrest him."

"How do you know he won't have a weapon?" Jeff asked.

Stacie stared at him. "I guess I don't, but what else can we do? He's stalking us, and the police won't help. Sooner or later he'll get to Julie or me and then what?" Her voice broke. "We can't live like that. I'd rather finish this on our terms, not his."

Jeff ran his hand over his eyes. "Okay, but we have to time this very carefully. No mistakes."

Stacie turned to Kyle. "What about you? Are you in?"

He squeezed her hand and nodded.

"What are you guys doing?" Julie asked.

The three of them jumped and looked at one another. "We are… um…" Jeff began. "We're discussing…"

Stacie hadn't expected Julie to come downstairs. They couldn't tell her the truth, not in her fragile state of mind. "We're discussing a project for school…for science class."

Jeff nodded in agreement. "Yeah, Kyle and I are doing a project together, and we asked Stacie to help."

Julie crossed her arms in front of her. "Really? Do you expect me to believe that? What are you planning? I know it has something to do with Jason Andrews."

Jeff stared at her, openmouthed. "You too?"

She shook her head. "Not like Stacie; I don't have visions, just premonitions. The night of the tornado, I thought I felt this way because of the approaching storm. I went out the back door to look at the sky and that's when he grabbed me." She sucked in a ragged breath. "So what are you planning?"

Stacie told her about the vision and their plan to record Jason Andrews in the act. "It sounds like a good plan, but what if he has the knife?"

All eyes turned to Stacie. She threw her hands up. "Okay, I admit it. He had a knife; but with Jeff and Kyle there and the police on the way, it'll be fine. He's not going to kill me in front of everyone. So far he's only guilty of kidnapping, not murder."

Jeff stood abruptly. "None that we know of." He shook his head. "That's it; forget it. It's too dangerous."

"I'm sorry, Stacie; I agree with Jeff." Kyle said. "You don't know what he might do."

Stacie looked from one face to the other. "All we have to do is make sure he doesn't grab me from behind, and I'll get him to confess to kidnapping Julie from the diner." She turned to Julie. "What do you think?"

Julie's eyes were wide and scared. Her chin trembled. "He's out there waiting right now, isn't he?" She sat at the table. "Stacie, you've always been the brave one, but I can't ask you to do this for me."

"It's not just for you," Stacie said. "We're both in danger. We have to stop him tonight. I'll get the camera if you'll wrap up the bag of trash. You can do the recording and call the police while I'm getting him to confess."

Julie nodded, and Stacie dashed into the other room for the camera. When she turned around, Kyle was there.

He took the camera out of her hand. "Okay, I'm in." He touched her cheek and slipped his hand behind her neck, drawing her closer until their bodies were almost touching. She was sure she was about to get her first kiss. Kyle leaned toward her. She closed her eyes.

"Hey, you two," Jeff said from the doorway. "Save it for later. If we're going to do this, then let's do it."

They jumped apart. Stacie giggled. Kyle grinned.

• • •

STACIE PICKED UP the trash bag and carried it out the door. The trash cans sat on the curb near the light on the corner of the block. She knew he was watching from between the neighbor's garage and house. She'd promised Jeff and Kyle she wouldn't give him a chance to sneak up behind her. They wanted him to confront her, thinking she'd be an easy target. Kyle had pretended to go home and was now hiding across the street, filming her. She had the small voice recorder she'd used in speech class last year in her jeans pocket as a backup.

She dropped the bag into the trash can and slapped down the lid. Her hand still gripped the trash can lid when suddenly he appeared in front of her with the knife.

He smiled. "I've been waiting for you, Julie."

Stacie gasped. "What do you want?"

"Why, Julie, I want you, of course. You left so abruptly from the cabin, we didn't get a chance to finish our little game." He was moving closer to her as he spoke.

He was close enough now that she could see his face for the first time. If it wasn't for his eyes, she would have found him attractive. But they were like looking into the eyes of a mannequin: completely blank. She shivered.

He moved closer as he spoke again. "Are you chilled? I shouldn't be keeping you out here in this night air."

He was so close. She could have reached out and touched him. Instead her fingers tightened on the metal trash can lid. "What do you want? I escaped from you once. I can do it again."

"Yes, you did. I don't know how, but you won't escape this time, Julie. I've found a new place. One that's much more private, and we can be together without any interruptions."

His hand reached out to grab her, and she swung the trash can lid into his face. "That one's for Julie."

He staggered backward. She stepped toward him and brought the lid across the other side of his face. "And that one's for me."

The knife flew out of his hand. He dropped to the ground. Jeff was on him before she had a chance to hit him again. He tied his hands behind him and kept one foot on his back.

The police were coming down the street with sirens and flashing lights.

Kyle came from the other side of the street, still recording but shut the camera off when he reached her. He stuck the little camera in his pocket. "You okay?" he whispered.

She nodded and looked into his eyes. All the emotions Jason Andrews lacked were in Kyle's smiling eyes. She grinned. "So are you ever going to kiss me or what?"

DONNA JEAN MCDUNN writes short stories and novels for young adults, and women's romance. She resides in Iowa, married at nineteen, had three daughters by the age of twenty-seven, and graduated from college at forty-two. Her first of eight grandchildren was born by age forty-five, and she earned her third degree black belt in Songahm Taekwondo at fifty-eight. Her first book, *Nightmares*, will be released in May 2013 from Muse It UP Publsihing.

To read more of her stories go to: www.storiesthatlift.com, www.bumples.com, www.knowonder.com/pack-leader-short-bedtime-stories, or www.thepinkchameleon.com. You can find her on Facebook and LinkedIn under her name, on twitter @DMcDunn, and read her blog: www.donnajeanmcdunn.wordpress.com.

It Is So Sweet

Pat Cox

THEY FOUND HER sitting on the tow path by the stream, her feet dangling in the swift-running water, staring into the distance as if lost in thought. Someone had reported to the police that she had been sitting there for at least three hours without moving; but of course no one had spoken to her, so it was up to us to sort it out! Nothing unusual, that's what most people do. Oh yes, you get the occasional person who helps, but in this mind-your-own-business world, it didn't concern them did it?

I walked up to her and said, "Hello," and she looked up at me, shading her eyes against the sun and smiled. "Hello," she replied, and continued dangling her feet in the water and staring at some point in the distance.

I squatted down beside her "Are you okay?"

She kept looking into the distance. "I'm fine. Isn't it lovely here?"

I nodded and looked at her; she didn't seem to have any shoes or bag with her and this worried me. My police radio crackled, and my partner, who was sitting in the car up on the road a few yards away, asked what was happening. I told him that I didn't seem to be getting anywhere and I didn't remember seeing a car parked on the road; could he see one?

I heard him get out of the patrol car and waited for his reply. Sergeant Cummings was a good sort and didn't moan when a WPC asked him to do something, especially in cases like this; it was easier to stretch your legs and look for the woman's car than deal with the woman herself!

"No car anywhere around here" came his reply. "What's happening now?"

I wish I knew as I remained squatting down beside this woman. "Can I ask your name?"

"Yes, you can."

"So, what is your name?"

"Don't you know?" she replied, looking at me, her eyes wide.

Oh dear, was this some celebrity publicity stunt, and I didn't recognize her? "No, I'm afraid I don't."

"Oh, you are a police woman?"

"Yes."

"Well, you're supposed to know everything, so you must know my name."

"Hang on, I'll call my sergeant; he may know. Where are your shoes?" She looked at her feet in the water. "What shoes?"

"Your shoes."

"But I don't have any shoes." Her eyes started to fill with tears. "Why don't I have any shoes?"

Cummings arrived at this point; in his fifties and pink in the face, he'd only been with me tonight because there was a football match at the local field, and they were expecting trouble. Normally he'd have been behind a desk in the control room but had been persuaded to partner me tonight because he thought it would be quieter on this out-of-town patrol than back at HQ!

"Hi, Sarge, this lady seems to think we should know who she is," I whispered to him, "and she says she doesn't have any shoes—and that's upset her."

He looked at me and shrugged his shoulders slightly. "What's the matter, love?" he asked as she sat there with tears running down her face. "What's wrong?"

She looked up at him and said, "I don't have any shoes."

He smiled at her. "That's no problem, love; we can take you home and get you some. Come on, let's get you in the car before your feet get too cold."

He put his hand out, and she took it and pulled her feet out of the water, and I saw that the skin was torn and grazed with bits of gravel embedded in the skin.

"Hang on, I'll get the firstaid kit and tidy your feet up; they look a bit sore." I glanced at Cummings, and he nodded as I ran up the bank to the car, grabbed the kit, and returned to the tow path.

I knelt down beside her, dried her feet, and put some antiseptic on them. She winced. "Sorry, just trying to make sure you don't get an infection," I said as I gently put pads over the worst bits and taped them up. "Right, let's get you up to the car; do you have a bag?"

She looked around, and again her eyes filled with tears. "I don't know."

Her lips quivered. "I can't remember. Do you know who I am?" She turned to Cummings. "She doesn't, I don't, do you?"

I looked over her head at him and raised my eyebrows; it looked like we had a case of amnesia.

Cummings smiled at her. "Well, let's see; I'm George Cummings, and this young lady is WPC Lucy Wells; and what I suggest we do is take you for a ride around and see if we can help you remember who you are." He took her arm gently; and with me on her other side, we helped her up the bank and into the car.

While the sergeant. settled her in the car, I quickly scouted either side of the road to see if there were any specks of blood—you know, like they do on those American CSI shows—to see if I could see which way she had come, since the condition of her feet showed she must have been bleeding for quite a while. But there wasn't a trace of blood anywhere.

I climbed into the car and strapped myself in as he started the engine. Sergeant Cummings looked at me and I shook my head; it seemed a bit strange there not being any blood, unless... "Did you walk along the tow path to get here?" I asked her, turning in my seat so that I could see her face. She shrugged her shoulders and looked out at the river.

We drove back along the road and took the main road to the police station on the outskirts of the town. I watched her look out the window as a child might when being driven by her parents. "Do you remember this road?"

"No, ummm—oh yes, that shop there sells ice cream. We always used to stop there and get one when we went down to the river."

I don't know what she was seeing, because all I could see was a boarded-up, dilapidated old shop with a FOR SALE sign on the front. "When was that?" I asked her.

"Whenever Daddy and Mummy had had a row. Daddy used to get his fishing rods out and take us fishing, but we liked the ice cream, and playing in the water."

"Didn't do much good for the fishing, you splashing about," Cummings commented.

"Oh, Daddy didn't seem to mind; and we'd stop and buy fish and chips on the way home, and he'd say, 'Here's some I caught earlier, and we used to laugh and tell him he'd never get a Blue Peter badge by cheating."

"Where's your daddy now?" It was a long shot, but I thought it was worth asking.

"I don't know; he went away when I was twelve, and Mummy was very cross." Tears started to run down her face again, and I tried to think of something else to ask her. "You said that your daddy took you to the river. Who else did he take?"

She smiled. "My sister. We used to have great fun there, but she went away to college." Her face dropped again. "I didn't see her again. She didn't like Mummy's new boyfriend. "

"When was that?" I asked, but she shrugged her shoulders and looked out the window.

"What was your sister's name?" I asked. She looked at me, and I could see she was trying to remember; but there was no reply.

By now we had arrived at the station, so we helped her in and took her through to an interview room. Not the one we use for suspects, but the nice one, where we talk to potential witnesses. It had a couple of comfortable chairs and a coffee table, as well as an interview table with chairs on either side. We helped her into the room and sat her in one of the armchairs. Then I went to make some tea. I wasn't sure if she took sugar or not, so I put some in a dish and put it on the tray with a spare spoon, and carried it back to the room.

Cummings took his mug and shoveled some sugar into it and said, "I'd better go and book this in," and wandered out of the room. I handed her a mug of tea and offered her the sugar, which she refused. I sat in the armchair opposite her and took off my cap. "That's better; that thing makes my head sweat when it's warm like today. We've been lucky this summer, haven't we? There hasn't been too much rain, but I expect we'll get some soon now that it's September."

She nodded and continued sipping her tea. "You've got a nice tan. Been on holiday?"

She smiled and said, "Yes, it was lovely holiday; we went caravanning in France. I've still got some francs left from my pocket money."

"Well, that didn't get me far," I thought, as she was obviously remembering a holiday from a long time ago. Francs indeed! "We went to Croatia; it's marvelous how they've rebuilt the country since the war—and it was quite cheap," I said, but she didn't seem to notice. In fact, the holiday had been last year, with my now ex-fiancé, Barry, the two-timing snake; but I'd hoped it might have stirred a memory or two—you know, all those UN troops and things.

I looked down at my finger and could still see a slight indentation where the ring had adorned it before I threw it back in his face, when an idea struck me. I looked at her fingers, and she had a signet ring on her right hand but a definite large, white band on her left hand where either a wide wedding ring or a wedding ring and an engagement ring had been.

"Where are your rings, love?"

She looked down at her finger, and her hand shook so much I thought she was going to drop the mug. "My wedding ring, where is it? Have you got it?"

I shook my head "No, love, I haven't. How long have you been married?"

She didn't answer as she stared down at her finger, and great big tears dripped on to her hand. "I can't remember, but I've lost my rings."

I pointed to the signet ring on her other hand and said, "You've still got that one. What's the pattern on the shield?"

She looked down at her ring and fiddled with it, and then put her hand out for me to see. It had a small diamond chip in one corner of the shield and a heart inscribed in the middle with a *W* and a *B* in it.

I asked her if I could take it off, and she shook her head. "It's too tight and won't come off." She tugged at it to demonstrate how tight it was.

Cummings came back in the room. He was having difficulty with the form, color of eyes, etc. so I left him with her and went to finish it.

"Oh, Sarge, that signet ring's got initials on it; try thinking of names beginning with *W*," I said as I left the room.

I finished the form: gray eyes, light-brown hair, about 5' 4", slim build, and no visible distinguishing marks. We needed to take her to the hospital. She needed those feet dressed properly, and a proper examination and assessment. We'd brought her here first because there had been a few fights after the match, and we didn't want to upset her any more than she already was.

No one had reported her missing, but it was early yet; to my knowledge she'd only been gone about five hours. Right, next stop hospital.

We arrived at the hospital without incident and were met by a specially trained nurse as I'd arranged. She took "Mrs. W."—as we had started calling her—into a cubicle. She went quietly. I had explained to her that she would have a full medical because it might help us find out who she was. I stood outside the cubicle in case I was needed. Cummings was back at the station tidying up the paperwork and looking through the missing person's lists. He'd also put out a bulletin in case she had abandoned her car somewhere along the road by the riverbank. Wish I'd thought of that, but I suppose that's what made him an experienced sergeant and me a constable. Still, you learn by example, I suppose.

The nurse reappeared after half an hour and drew me to one side. "Apart from her feet being in a bad condition and the memory loss, there's nothing wrong with her. No bruises or cuts, and she hasn't been raped. I've put a call out for a psychiatrist to come and see her, but it may take some time as it is Saturday."

I thanked the nurse and called out to Mrs. W., "Can I come in?"

She didn't reply, so I popped my head around the curtain and she was sitting there on the side of the bed in a hospital gown, her feet expertly bound up. She had been crying, and I offered her a tissue from the box that the nurse had left by the bed. She took it and wiped her eyes.

"Let's get you back into bed; a doctor will be in to talk to you."

"Don't leave me, please!" she burst out. "The nurse didn't know who I was either or where my shoes were."

I sighed; it looked as if it was going to be a long afternoon, but I mustered a smile and put my hand on her shoulder. "Never mind, the doctor will be here soon. He may be able to help you find out. I'll get you a cup of tea."

She nodded, and I got her settled back in the bed. I went to find a tea machine, curious to see what type of brown liquid it would dispense. As I came back with two cups of nearly drinkable tea, there was a sudden burst of activity. Two rather drunk football hooligans were brought in under guard. Both had blood pouring from wounds on their heads and were making a lot of noise. I hurried back to the cubicle in case they had alarmed Mrs. W. Sure enough she was cowering, squatting on the floor by the head of the bed.

I reassured her and got her back in the bed, putting her cup of tea on the trolley the nurse had left beside her bed. I noticed that every time those guys shouted, Mrs. W. flinched.

Finally the psychiatrist turned up. I left the cubicle to radio in a report of what was happening and got reminded that I'd broken protocol by not taking a DNA swab or her fingerprints. I explained that there was a lot of noise in the hospital because of the drunks from the match, but I planned to do it next, which they were quite happy about.

I grabbed another cup of that stuff that passed for tea from the machine and went back to my post. I could hear the doc talking to her and her replies and tears, but it sounded as if they weren't getting anywhere. More football casualties were arriving, and the noise was horrendous for a hospital. I who was used to noise even found it beginning to hurt my ears. At one point I found myself stopping a lad who was starting to get aggressive with one of the nurses.

The doc popped his head around the curtain and beckoned to me. "I'm going to give her something to calm her down and get her up in the ward for some more tests. Where did you find her?"

I gave him the rundown on what had happened and told him about the need for fingerprints and a DNA swab, and he agreed to get a nurse to help me once she'd had the injection and was up in the ward.

I arrived back at the station long after my shift had ended and handed over the sample and fingerprint card and signed out. At least the overtime would come in handy, I thought as I climbed on my bike and cycled home. I knew that the boys who dealt with the samples had long since gone home, and they probably wouldn't be dealt with till Monday, as the case didn't seem to be connected to any violent crime.

Sunday was quiet. I suppose most of the ne'er-do-wells were nursing hangovers from yesterday, and I was back with my original partner, PC Brian Collins, who was nursing a black eye from the problems yesterday. Of course I did the usual ribbing about his wife blacking his eye, but it was only in joke. He'd been married about ten years, and he and his wife were finally expecting their first baby. They had often invited me round for a bite to eat, and they had asked me if I'd like to be godparent to "Master X," as they were calling him after the scan definitely showed that the baby was a boy.

We got back after our shift, and I asked if there had been any news on Mrs. W. but there wasn't, so I cycled back to my flat and thought no more of it. I'd just made myself some supper—bacon and eggs—when my mobile rang. It was Cummings. "Lucy, love, can I come round?"

I thought it was a bit strange but replied yes, and he hung up. I looked around my scruffy little flat and spotted that bag that I should have dumped yesterday, so I grabbed it and ran down to the basement.

One thing, in fact the only good thing, about this block of old-fashioned flats was that the heating came with the rent and was run from an old boiler in the basement; and although we weren't supposed to do this—but we all did—I quickly chucked the bag into the boiler and my overflowing rubbish bin into the communal dustbins down there before heading back up the stairs. I'd just got back in the flat and was trying to eat my half-cold meal when the doorbell rang. I answered it and up the stairs puffed Cummings, still in uniform; but I wasn't sure of his shift pattern that day. I thought he was back on the communications.

He came in and sat down, breathing heavily. "You really ought to get more exercise," I said to him as he regained his breath. "Do you want a cuppa?"

He nodded, but there was something not quite right; he had a worried look in his eyes. "I'll make the tea, love," he said. "You finish your meal."

It was really cold and congealed by then, so I laughed and said something about being on a diet and took it into the kitchen to dump in my now-empty rubbish bin while Cummings put on the kettle. I ended up making the tea—he couldn't find anything—and we took it back into the living room. Well, it was a bed/sitting room really, but I'd put screens around one end to divide the bed off from the rest of the room. "Sit down, love." he said. "I've got something to tell you."

Worried now by his attitude, I sat and watched him as he took a sip of tea. "It's like this: that woman we found yesterday, well, we've found her car. A patrol noticed it standing there on Saturday night; but as it's a spot known for naughty goings-on, they didn't think any more about it. But it was still there this morning as they finished their shift, so they got out to have a look. It was unlocked, and a handbag was inside with a driver's license in the name of Wendy Jane King. The registration came back as being hers as well."

I gulped. "Wwwwendy King, bbbbut that's the name of Barry's wife!" I stammered—I do that when I'm upset. "So wwwwhat happened"

Cummings took another sip of his tea. "We're not sure; but when we went knocking on their door, it was open, and there was King lying on the kitchen floor in a pool of blood. He'd been stabbed."

I felt shaky. Okay, I mean, the bloke had been a two-timing, double-dealing snake, but to hear that he had been found like that was a hell of a shock! I must have gone white, because Cummings took his hip flask out and tried to pour some whiskey in my tea. I put my hand over my cup. I didn't want any alcohol; I just wanted to be alone.

"I'll be okay. It's just a bit of a shock. I mean, I haven't seen him for nearly a year. I'll be all right. Just let me get my head around it, and I'll be all right tomorrow," I said, and stood up.

Cummings patted my shoulder, asked if I needed anything, and said that I should call if I wanted some company. Then he let himself out of the flat, shutting the door quietly behind him.

For once I was glad I was not in the section house. At least I had some peace and quiet to gather my thoughts. This place was expensive and took half my salary each month, but for once it didn't matter.

Barry had persuaded me to lease this place—just for a while, he'd said. Then we'd move to somewhere better and prettier—well, he had. But I was still stuck here with the two-year lease that I'd optimistically signed eighteen months ago, and it was making a big hole in my bank balance each month. He'd never paid his half but had bought the groceries each week in cash, so it didn't really matter.

What I hadn't realized at the time was that if he'd set up a standing order on his joint bank account, it would show up; but by paying his expenses in cash each week, no one was the wiser. Were they?

And now he was dead, stabbed.

Well, his wife couldn't have done it. We'd found no sign of blood on her, apart from her feet, and that was her own. There was no sign of any blood in the car that they found. But where were her rings?

I smiled to myself, "Well, Barry, you've got your comeuppance," I thought, and went to cook some more bacon and eggs, as I was hungry now.

The next morning I went back to work and asked how the case was going. The uniforms didn't seem to know a lot, as it had been handed over to CID. All my lot were doing were the house-to-house inquiries.

I went up to the CID room and spoke to DS Winters and told him that I knew the deceased but had never met his wife, and how and why I knew him. He took a statement from me, and I signed it. I told him I hadn't seen Barry since November last year, when I'd thrown my engagement ring back at him and told him I never wanted to see him again. I'd actually said a lot more than that, but I kept that to myself. I think they knew I'd cut out the expletives, but they didn't seem to mind.

They told me that, as I had some vague connection to the case, I couldn't help on the house-to-house, nor could I visit Wendy in the hospital. I nodded and went back downstairs to where Brian Collins was waiting for me. He took the keys to the patrol car, and we went off, assigned to keep an eye out for shoplifters.

We had the usual tear-aways and managed to arrest one man who looked like he was part of the gang that was operating in the area. We also managed to get his van that was full of stolen goods. The beat bobby would keep an eye out for the rest of them while we took him back to the station and arranged to have the van towed away for examination. He caught two more as they were looking for the van, so between us we had a good morning.

We went to the garage to look at the van. Inside it were a few thousand pounds worth of high-end shoes, handbags, and clothes. Collins remarked that we'd saved the insurance company a few quid there, and I nodded; but my attention was on the red mini standing in splendid isolation while forensics pulled it apart to check for blood, etc.

It was a bright red, six-months old, top-of-the-line car. The kind I'd always wanted but couldn't afford because of the flat. It so wasn't fair, but what good would it do her now, I wondered. I realized Collins had been talking to me, and I apologized and told him about the car and the woman. He'd heard all the gossip and could understand my interest.

"Come on, at least dumping him when you did means that you're not involved." He laughed as we went back up the stairs, leaving the clothes in boxes by the lift. We'd get them when the lift was repaired, no point in trying to carry them.

The shoplifting gang leader took up most of the rest of our shift, and he insisted that he didn't know anything about the clothes, yadda, yadda, yadda; but we knew we'd got this one bang to rights. His "assistants" who had been picked up turned out to be illegal immigrants, and were happy to confess because he hardly paid them anything for their *work*. It was their way of getting revenge.

Revenge, such a sweet word. I suppose that with Barry getting stabbed, I'd got mine at last! But I put that thought away and continued filling in all those forms, then popped back up to the CID to see if there was anything new.

There was. Apparently a nosy neighbor had seen a white van draw up outside the Kings' house, and a slim, young lad in a black jumpsuit had gotten out and spoken with Barry, who was under the bonnet of his green BMW. She'd seen them walk around the back and then the youngster—he was only a skinny little lad— had come back out clutching a newspaper, got back into the van,. and drove off. She thought that it was a bit unusual but didn't seem to realize that she might have seen the murderer. Well, it was either him or Wendy.

The old dear seemed to spend half her time nosing around her net curtains and was sure she'd never seen this person before; but she described him as slim, quite young, about 5' 6" tall, with long, straggly dark hair under a baseball cap pulled low over his face.

Then she'd gone on to say that about ten minutes later, that "nice Mrs. King" had come rushing out of the house and gotten in to her car and driven off. She hadn't seen her husband for the rest of the day, nor did Mrs King's car come back. But as she didn't like to interfere, she hadn't rung us, because last time she'd rung to complain, some snotty-nosed constable had told her she was wasting police time. Well, she wasn't to know that the kid climbing in through that window was a mate of the son of the house who had lost his keys, so his mate had offered to climb up, as he was more agile than he.

We all remembered who that "snotty-nosed constable" was; he'd had his card marked several times for this type of thing and was now working for a security firm on car park control.

Anyway, the old dear gave the house-to-house mob a good description of this young lad; but she hadn't been able to see his eyes, nor had she thought to get the registration of the van. They called up all the CCTV footage for the time she said; but the description of a smallish white van could fit a lot of vehicles, and several had been spotted—near a car valet place as well as—all over town.

They'd gone round there, but quite honestly, the lads didn't have enough brains between them to help. They had had three white vans in on Saturday; all were regulars. They gave the constables the details they had, which was basically just the name and what type of clean they'd given them; and no, they hadn't seen any blood in any of them. So that line of inquiry had drawn a blank, especially as one had been driven by a woman.

Tuesday came and went, and there was no news from the investigation. The house-to-house and other inquiries continued. The mini had no signs of blood or anything incriminating in it, nor had Wendy's handbag; but on Wednesday, all hell broke loose.

She had regained her memory and had screamed so much that they sedated her before CID could ask her any questions. They had to put her in a side ward now, Cummings told me confidentially.

Apparently, she was allowed to get up and have a shower; and on her way to the bathroom, she spotted a newspaper being read by one of the other patients. On the front page was a picture of her husband, and she had stood stock-still and screamed: "Barry, all that blood, Barry, NO!" then fallen to the floor, screaming and crying.

The nurses had called the psychiatrist and put her in a vacant side ward. She had kept on screaming the same thing over and over again, so the staff had no option but to sedate her; and now CID was kicking its heels, waiting to interview her. So that's what Wendy looked like. I had never seen her before, not even a photo. I think I remarked something like "Well, at least we know who she is, poor thing," and I meant it. It wasn't her fault that her dead husband had been a two-timing snake, and I thought that she was better off without him. But of course, I didn't voice my thoughts. How could I?

Over the next few days they patiently interviewed Wendy. She didn't remember me or how she had gotten to the hospital, but slowly her story came out. It was a Saturday, and for once she didn't have to work. Because of the football match, her boss at the agency had decided to close and board up the shop. These local derbies always had the chance of turning violent. So she'd slept in and cooked Barry a nice breakfast. He did like his bacon and eggs. When he went out to check the bits on his car ready for next week's breakaway in the Lake District, she had put the plates in to soak and took off her rings, because "the new engagement ring Barry gave me last year was a bit big and would get caught in the rubber gloves."

She remembered the glasses that he'd brought upstairs the night before, and the bottle, and decided that they ought to come down to be washed up as well. So she had padded upstairs in her bare feet and, for some reason, thought that she should shower and get dressed, which she did. As she had gotten dressed, she thought she heard Barry talking rather loudly on the phone, telling someone to "Piss off and forget it." He did get annoyed when people rang him on his day off about trivial work matters, apparently. Then she heard the back door slam, so she thought he had gone back out to the car and came downstairs, forgetting the wineglasses and bottle. It was confirmed that they had been left on the floor outside the bathroom—and now they knew why.

She had walked through to the kitchen and saw Barry lying there on the floor and all this blood, and she couldn't remember anything more until she saw his photo in the paper that morning. The psychiatrist had said that this was normal, and she may never remember how she had run out of the house and driven off. Instinctively going to a place of safety and past happiness.

· · ·

THEY NEVER DID find the killer, and now, ten years later as a DS, I've been asked to go through some of the cold cases from that year; and as I opened the box with all the files and paper clippings in it, the memories come flooding back.

The case was in the papers for a few weeks and got resurrected when Wendy, after being discharged from the hospital after a few months, put the house on the market. She went to stay with her sister, who had contacted the police when she saw Wendy's picture in one of the national newspapers. I hear she finally recovered and got married again just recently.

They never found the van or her rings or, strangely enough, the rubber gloves. I smiled to myself as I pulled out the interview statement. The old lady is long gone, so we can't interview her again—wouldn't want to anyway. The white van she mentioned is probably rotting in a scrap yard now, but it was so nice of my neighbor to lend it to me to get my shopping in each Saturday morning. I didn't have to pay for petrol either. I just had to get it valeted once a month for him.

It was a handy deal I'd set up a few months earlier—so were the dust sheets and the extra steering wheel cover that I'd managed to get hold of—that meant that any blood left on me would be absorbed by them. That boiler was so handy for disposing of them, the jumpsuit, overshoes, and the newspaper that I'd used to cover up the blood on the front of the jumpsuit. I had always used the name Barbara Smith at the valet place.

The rubber gloves went the same way too—well, it stopped any blood from getting on my hands. As for the wedding ring, that went the same way as the knife: right into the waterfall where the stream met the river, and has never been found. I grew my hair long again; it didn't need to be so short anymore. People said it suited me.

The engagement ring I still have; how dare he give it to Wendy—it was mine, the one I'd thrown back in his face when I had found him out! It's still tucked in the back of one drawer in the chest in the bedroom of my new little house that I bought. It doesn't cost as much as the rent I had been paying on that awful flat all those years ago.

It was a shame that Wendy had been at home. I had banked on her being at work as she usually was on a Saturday morning; and since I'd never seen her, I didn't realize who she was until I saw that signet ring. But even that worked out all right in the end; she's better off without that two-timing snake, Barry. If only she knew that!

"Yes," I thought as I put the files back and put the box to go back into the archives, "revenge is so sweet."

PAT COX retired from working for The Royal British Legion two years ago and discovered that she likes writing and history. She still supports the charity and her many grandchildren as well. She has two sites: https://madkentdragon.wordpress.com, which contains local history and political comment, and htpps://madkentdragonstories.wordpress.com, where her stories live.

More Books from Buddhapuss Ink

Mystery / Thrillers

The Last Track: A Mike Brody Novel
by Sam Hilliard

Imagine if being late meant a child disappeared forever. That is the fear that drives Mike Brody: the man you want, when the one you love is missing. Mike is more than just a master tracker. An ex-Special Forces operative, Smoke jumper, and now extreme adventure tour guide, he also possesses a unique ability to tap into the memory and emotional state of those he pursues.

In *The Last Track*, a police detective recruits Mike to help find an asthmatic boy lost in the dense woods surrounding a dude ranch in Montana. An unwitting murder witness, the boy burrows ever deeper into the rugged terrain, fearful of being found. As Mike and a local officer search for the boy, the killer follows them. While the investigation expands, his ex-wife, a well-connected journalist, uses her contacts to unravel the truth behind the murder. Her discoveries threaten to snare them all in a treacherous conspiracy…

Mike Brody: Some say his gift is supernatural; others consider it a curse. To Mike Brody, it's a penance.

Available in paperback and kindle editons.

Mystery Times Ten 2011

Chosen from more than 200 submissions, these ten mystery short stories come from new and established authors alike. Never before published, they are gathered together in our first annual *Mystery Times* YA collection.

This collection includes Barb Goffman's *Truth and Consequences*–nominated for the 2012 Agatha, Anthony and Macavity Short Story Awards!

There is something here for every YA mystery fan, from hard-boiled to paranormal. Each story is a small bite of mystery that will satisfy and delight even the most discerning of readers. So sit down and dip in.

We guarantee you won't be able to stop with just one!

Available in paperback and kindle editons.

Contemporary Fiction / Romance

The Stone Trilogy
by Mariam Kobras

The saga of Jon Stone, international rock superstar, and the woman
he loved, lost, and found again
Available in paperback and kindle editions.

The Distant Shore, Book I
Winner 2012, Independent Publishers' Book Award

There's nothing like finding a letter on your breakfast
table from a teenage son you knew nothing about, but
that's what happens to international rock star Jon Stone. He
drops everything to find the boy and his mother, the girl he
loved so many years ago who left him when his rock 'n' roll
life became too much for her to bear.

Seeing her is like falling in love all over again, and everything seems
perfect until someone sets out to destroy their idyllic life.

Under the Same Sun, Book II

There comes a time in life when you realize that neither
fame nor wealth will carry the day. It's the moment when all
that matters are love and faith.

Stand with Naomi on a lonely beach as she faces her
greatest threat and discovers that nothing is more important
than her love for Jon.

Emerging Voices Imprint—Coming Soon!

Sweet William
by Martie Odell Ingebretsen

When William is arrested on suspicion of child molestation,
it is the catalyst that finally puts him back on the road to
recovery. For too long he was caught in a web of guilt that
turned him from the owner of a successful chain of gas
stations and loving family man into a homeless alcoholic
who spent his time dreaming. What appears to be just one
more bit of bad luck turns out to be the tipping point that allows him to
open the door to the past and at long last, accept it and the love of the
people around him. Slowly, life welcomes William back, and he is ready to
embrace it once more.